Raven's Woman

MARIAM KIRBY

Raven's Woman
Copyright © 2021 Mariam Kirby

ISBN 978-1-7352249-4-7

Library of Congress Control Number:

This is a work of fiction. Names, characters,
places and incidents are either the product of the
author's imagination or are used fictitiously, and
any resemblance to actual persons, living or dead,
businesses, institutions, organizations, events,
or locales is entirely coincidental.

First Edition

10 9 8 7 6 5 4 3 2

Printed in the United States of America

For Monica Mari,
and for her old, old friend,
Pepper.

One

Catherine O'Shea's mood was as gloomy as the gray afternoon sky over her head. Her shoulders sagged as she watched the veterinarian's truck drive away from the front gate. With the vet's bill clutched in her hand, she did some quick mental arithmetic. The cost of the vet's visit added to the cost of new therapeutic horseshoes for her buckskin gelding made Catherine want to cry. The gelding was the only horse in her stable that she actually owned. The bills were hers alone and couldn't be passed on to a client. Worse, she hadn't been in the horse training business long enough to build up her savings account, and there was no way she would borrow the money. Not that a bank would consider lending her any. Her finances were stretched to the limit, and her income barely covered her monthly expenses. She would have to scrimp on things for herself for the next six months, things like the new saddle she had been hoping to buy. With a feeling close to dread, she thought about the bills that would be coming due soon, and went back to work.

By late afternoon, the horses in her care had been fed, exercised, groomed, and bedded down in a clean barn. Usually, by this time of day, Catherine felt satisfied with all that she had accomplished. Today, she felt a tension headache lurking at the back of her neck. She swallowed a couple of over-the-counter pain tablets and drank a cup of leftover coffee. Then, only because she had promised a new client that she would, Catherine hitched a trailer to her truck so she could move the man's horse to her stable. She needed the added income more than ever, now.

Catherine tried to think of nothing at all as she drove on the narrow mountain road across the San Francisco Peninsula, headed to a farm that overlooked the Pacific Ocean. Once there, the client's young Thoroughbred stood stiff-legged at the bottom of the ramp that led into her trailer and refused to budge. After gentle persuasion failed to move the stubborn animal, Catherine wrapped a rope around its haunches, dug in her heels, and dragged the horse up the ramp. Sweating and completely out of patience, she started for home to the sound of iron-shod hooves pounding the trailer's tailgate. Minutes later, she drove into a winter downpour which made her slow the truck's speed to a crawl. Catherine peered into the falling rain and felt more disgust than sympathy for the half-wild horse trapped in the trailer as it fishtailed in the storm winds behind her pickup.

Billy Raven asked himself, probably for the hundredth time, why he had insisted that the band move into a mansion hidden on top of a California mountain. Despite his best efforts, the remote location had done nothing to unite the group. Cherokee's problems were as bad as ever. Arguments seemed to rise with the morning sun and last long after nightfall. If anything, the four men were turning from friends into enemies.

The band had converted the mansion's huge recreation room into a temporary recording studio. A jumble of mic stands, guitars, amplifiers, an electronic keyboard, and a drum kit surrounded the pool table in the center of the room. Black electrical cables snaked in all directions. In the center of the room, high-tech audio equipment covered the pool table's green felt surface. Overhead, a trio of Tiffany lamps shivered in time to the sound of drums and guitars blasting from the digital recorder.

The music fell far short of Cherokee's most recent album, and not anywhere near the quality of the band's first album. Acclaimed as one of America's top rock bands Billy wanted to keep it that way. While the songs played on, the tension in Billy's jaw cranked up another notch. Searching for patience he didn't feel, he stared up past the glittering glass lamps at the plaster fleurs-de-lis and fat cherubs that decorated the vaulted ceiling. The words tasteless and ostentatious didn't do the room justice.

Billy shook his head in disgust and turned to gaze at the view framed by the room's French doors.

Beyond the flagstone terrace, tree-covered hillsides stepped down in a massive staircase toward San Francisco Bay. Far below, the lights of rush hour traffic streamed in red and white comet trails across one of the bridges that linked the San Francisco Peninsula to cities on the eastern shore. Heavy rain, which had threatened throughout the gloomy afternoon, began to fall.

Across the room, fragrant oak logs blazed in a cavernous white marble fireplace. The other members of Cherokee lounged on matching leather sofas angled in front of the fire. The actions of the three men over the past two weeks had drained Billy of most of his self-control.

Now he struggled against his anger and forced his knotted hands to flex and relax. The band put up with one temperamental musician already, and John, as edgy as he was talented, pushed the limits as often as he could. Billy didn't intend to follow John's example. There was no need for an angry tirade.

The flaws in Cherokee's music hit like a fist in the face. The music itself would make his point more convincingly than any words could.

The clink of glass on glass drew Billy's notice. He frowned as Rick set his empty beer bottle on the coffee table, hooked another, then settled into the sofa cushions with the full bottle resting on his belt buckle. Then, Rick stretched his legs out toward the fire and crossed his ankles.

In counterpoint to Rick's lazy posture, John sat rigidly straight, his stare fixed on the floor. The corners of Billy's mouth lifted in a grim smile. He and John had been friends for years. In all that time, neither had backed away from an argument.

Billy's attention shifted to the fourth member of the band. Carl's massive form bulged from the second sofa like the buttress of a medieval fort. With casual disregard, the big man flicked the ash from his cigarette toward a priceless jade bowl lodged between his feet; the ashes missed the bowl and scattered on the Persian carpet.

Casual disregard was a theme that ran through everything the band had attempted in recent months. And Billy had reached his limit. Steeling himself for the battle to come, he snapped off the recording.

The sudden silence felt ominous. Billy realized that he was holding his breath. On a sigh, he waited for the others to make the next move. The staccato slap of rain falling from the mansion's eaves onto the stone terrace filled a long, uneasy pause.

Finally, Rick said, "Yeah, you're right. This is crap."

Billy waited. When nothing more was said, he challenged, "So, what are you going to do about it?"

"We're here, aren't we?" John's ruined voice was harsh as a file grating across rusted iron. His self-satisfied expression seemed at odds with the start of a quarrel.

"For how long?" Billy demanded.

John shot back, "What's that supposed to mean?"

"You want me to spell it out?" Billy stalked toward John. "We've lost our edge, our music stinks, and all you want to do is get laid."

John launched off the sofa. "Son of a bitch!"

The punch he aimed at Billy missed as Carl leaned forward and trapped the blow in a hand the size of a catcher's mitt. Undeterred, John snatched a vase full of flowers off of the coffee table and heaved it at the fireplace.

Crystal disintegrated against marble, raining blood-red roses and shards of glass onto the hearth.
"Very nice, John." Rick's ironic drawl slid across the scene. "Billy," he said, "be reasonable. Sometimes you get into a slump. It just happens."

"Hitting every club in San Francisco, then dragging your butts back here at noon, is not a slump," Billy wasn't in the mood for excuses, particularly lame ones.

John stood face to face, inches in front of Billy. "Nobody's locking me up on this godforsaken mountain for the next month."

Rick hauled John away from Billy. "Everybody chill. We gotta work things out."

John shook off Rick's hand and dropped one hip onto the arm of the nearest sofa. "While you work things out, Ricky boy, I'll just sit here like some starstruck groupie and let Billy run my life."

"No one's trying to run anyone's life," Billy snapped. "The band's in trouble. If we don't focus 24/7 on our music, we're history."

"That's real dramatic, Billy." John brushed an invisible speck from the glossy surface of the white leather pants that hugged his thighs. "Cherokee is a partnership. You don't own me, you don't give me orders."

"John's right," Carl's grim baritone rumbled. "You may be the founder of Cherokee, but it's three to one." "Is that how you all see it?" Billy asked.

The men's silence served as their answer. Defeated and furious, Billy stalked from the room. In the foyer, he paused just long enough to grab a jacket off a bench and shrugged it on. It was Carl's coat. It fit like a duffel bag, but he found the keys to Carl's Porsche in one pocket. The metal bit into his palm as he closed his fist around the keys, sealing his sudden decision to drive along Skyline Boulevard to a place where he could park and watch the storm smash everything in its path.

Outside, the light from the mansion's windows disappeared behind a curtain of ice-cold rain. Billy sprinted across the gravel drive and scrambled into the Porsche. The tires blasted a torrent of small stones as he gunned the sports car onto the country road that led to the scenic highway. Barely able to see beyond the rain hammering the windshield, Billy's anger drove him forward.

His closest friends had betrayed him. None of them seemed to share his vision of Cherokee's future. Every time he stood center stage and sang the lyrics to music he had written, he felt a strange mixture of power and vulnerability. It brought him joy. Nothing could make him shortchange himself, or the crowds who came to Cherokee's concerts. Somehow he'd get the band back on track. In the meantime, he planned to put a few miles between himself and the others so he could get a grip and not punch out anyone he might want to work with in the near future.

⁂

The growing storm caught Catherine still on the road at sundown. Each shift in the wind brought another violent downpour. The truck's headlights reflected back into her eyes from the falling rain and blurred the road ahead. Catherine squinted into the darkness and clung to the steering wheel the way a drowning woman might cling to a life preserver.

Even driving slowly, the truck's tires slid on the wet pavement and squealed around every curve in the narrow mountain road. The pickup shuddered as the trailer lurched from side to side at the whim of the wind. Catherine began to wonder if she should stop and wait for the storm to pass toward the east.

Tired and stressed by the events of the day, the thought of sitting in her truck for what could be several hours seemed beyond awful. She knew the road. She'd driven through the mountains to the seacoast several times over the summer, tempted by the wild romance of secluded beaches. There, lulled by the sound of waves, she spent hours searching for pieces of brightly colored sea glass among the pebbles at the ocean's edge.

Every visit to the beach had been a reward she gave herself for long days of hard physical labor. Last summer, she felt happy and full of hope. Today, with her dream of owning a training stable true at last, hope was limited to earning enough money to put food on the table, after paying for orthopedic horseshoes. Catherine groaned and decided to keep driving.

A few minutes later, she drove onto the long, straight section of pavement, which meant she was nearing the end of her trip. The thought wasn't especially comforting. In slightly more than half an hour she would be home and faced with another battle as she moved the immovable horse from the trailer into a stall in her barn. She imagined having to drag the creature out into the rain in a tug of war that would leave both of them wet and shivering with cold. And she would have to rub down the pigheaded beast before she could dry off herself. The prospect of an unpleasant evening furrowed her brow in a deep frown.

Suddenly, brilliant lights blinded her. She blinked to clear her vision and saw a small car speeding straight at her. The car's headlights rode low to the ground, but as the car topped a slight rise in the road, the lights struck her windshield again. Distracted by her anxious thoughts, Catherine had allowed her truck to drift into the oncoming lane.

At the last possible moment, Catherine jerked the steering wheel to the right. As her truck lurched back into its lane, she watched the sports car skid out of control.

The Porsche came to rest with its nose touching the low stone wall that separated traffic from a fatal drop down the mountainside. The sight of pitch black, rain-filled sky that stretched away in a bottomless expanse beyond the wall made Billy's skin crawl. His guts twisted into a queasy knot.

On its last spin, with the tires sliding in slow motion through deep mud, the Porsche had hit the wall. The headlight on that side was out. Billy swore under his breath and stepped from the car. His feet sank into muck up to his ankles. In less than a minute, the downpour soaked through his borrowed jacket. He swore louder and more creatively as he made his way to the front of the little car and peered at the headlight. The glass was smashed all to hell. As he leaned closer, his feet slipped and he reached out to catch himself. His hand hit the shattered headlight. The broken glass carved a gash at the base of his thumb. Soaking wet, muddy, and bleeding, he turned to look at the truck's driver.

The stupid girl could have killed him. The terrified expression on her stark white face was the last thing he saw before he was forced to drive the Porsche off the road. Billy wondered if she might have recognized him in the brief moment they stared at each other by the harsh light of colliding headlights. He thought not, because she still sat in her truck instead of bounding out into the storm and throwing herself at him in frenzied teenage adoration. Carl's huge coat and barrels of rainwater made a useful disguise, it seemed.

He stared at the girl through narrowed eyes. Her reckless driving had caused the accident, but she didn't seem to care enough to get out of her truck and ask if he was okay. Or to apologize.

The ache in his hand reminded him that he was bleeding. Smoldering with righteous indignation, Billy followed the path lit by the Porsche's single headlight through the mud to the girl's truck. She sat staring straight ahead as if hypnotized, or paralyzed. Or really scared, he thought. Even so, Billy wasn't in a sympathetic mood. He rapped his knuckles hard against the window beside her.

The girl's slim body jerked at the sound. Slowly, she unwound her fingers from the steering wheel and let her hands drop into her lap. Finally, she turned to look at him. He stepped into the glow of the truck's lights so she could appreciate how wet and pissed off he was.

The wind whipped his long, black hair forward in tangles across lean cheeks shadowed by dark whiskers. He clutched at a coat that covered him like the sagging skin of a very wet, very scruffy bloodhound. The jeans he wore were faded nearly white at the knees. He looked to Catherine like a street corner panhandler.

Catherine's eyes rose to his face. He lifted a hand and slicked his sopping hair off his forehead, revealing stark, angular features with all the softness of a pile of rocks. They provided a habitat for the eyes of a predator: intent, patient, full of menace. He took three, slow, menacing steps that brought him back beside her window.

Suddenly, Catherine felt furious. What right did this imbecile have to try to set a land speed record on a country road at night in a downpour? she fumed.

She yanked the handle and shoved the truck's door open—smack into the man's chest.

Billy held his ground against the pressure of the door and said, "Maybe you should move your truck back onto the road and turn off the engine."

Catherine looked around and gasped. Her pickup sat tipped to one side halfway off the pavement. Beneath the rattle of rain on the truck's roof, she heard the steady drone of the engine idling. She didn't remember shifting the gears into neutral, or pulling on the hand brake. She recalled the squeal of brakes, and then...

"The colt!" Catherine slammed the truck into gear and drove forward onto the pavement. She killed the engine and kicked her door all the way open. She snatched up her flashlight, leaped out of the truck, and rushed back to check on the horse trapped in her trailer.

The idiot whose stupidity could have killed her stood in the middle of the road. She aimed the flashlight at his face. "If my horse has fallen, I'll murder you!" she shouted, then turned the flashlight's beam onto the trailer's tailgate. From within, Catherine heard the reassuring sound of hooves shuffling on the thick rubber mat that covered the trailer's floor. She took hold of the tailgate, hoisted herself up and hooked her arms over the top. She swept the light forward. The colt arched his head over his shoulder to stare at her and stamped his feet in annoyance.

Billy stared after the girl. First, she forced his car off the road and into a rock wall. Just now, she nearly ran him over, and would have, if he didn't have great reflexes that let him dodge out of the way. She had all the competence of a complete pinhead. Still, she seemed extremely worried about her horse. So worried he started to feel alarmed himself. "Is your horse okay?"

The man had followed her to the back of the trailer. Catherine released her grip on the tailgate and dropped with a thud as her boots struck the ground. She clenched her teeth against the names she wanted to call him.

"Yes," she answered. She aimed her flashlight at his face, which made him him squint. "No thanks to you." She elbowed past him and marched back to the truck.

He caught up with her as she hustled inside and grabbed hold of the door, before she could slam it in his face. He held the door open with one hand and loomed over her, while icy rain poured in around him and drenched her jeans. The truck's interior lights glittered in his dark gaze. He didn't look the least bit contrite. "If you had kept going straight," he said, "I would have missed you by a mile."

Outraged, Catherine demanded, "What are you talking about?"

"Your truck turned, but the trailer kept coming right at me. You ran me off the road."

"And you almost hit me head-on at a hundred miles an hour! Do you think I was going to wait to see if you missed?"

"Apparently not." He looked over his shoulder at the sports car mired in the mud. "Good thing a Porsche turns on a dime, isn't it?"

"Don't you dare try to blame me. You were speeding."

"You were driving over the center line."

Pointing toward the rain-slick pavement, Catherine said, "Take a look. There is no center line."

"Well, if there had been a center line," he said, "you would have been driving on the wrong side of it." His eyes held hers. She looked away.

Faced with the truth, Catherine conceded, "Okay, so I was out of my lane a little. Trucks drift sideways in high winds. But you were going way too fast."

"Yeah. I wasn't thinking about oncoming traffic. I didn't expect any during a storm like this. I should have dropped my speed a bit."

"A bit?"

Billy didn't like the girl's tone. "Don't push your luck, kid. We've both admitted some responsibility." He rubbed the tender spot on his jaw where his well-known face had connected with the Porsche's steering wheel.

"What's wrong with your hand?" she asked.

He shoved his hand deep into his jacket pocket. "Nothing."

"There's blood on your face. It wasn't there a minute ago. Let me see."

His hand stayed where he'd hidden it. He didn't want her fussing over him. He considered the cut payback for getting behind the wheel of a car when he felt angry and frustrated. He began to move away.

Catherine grabbed the front of his coat and tugged. "You aren't going anywhere until I see your hand."

He pried her hands loose. Then he smiled down at her and she supposed she'd never seen a smile before. All other smiles were pale counterfeits compared to the sensuous curve of lips and flash of teeth that transformed his face. He held her hands in both of his and she forgot to look for the source of blood on his fingers. She gazed at him and thought the rain and wind must have stopped, she felt so warm all of a sudden.

"I need to get the Porsche out of the mud."

He was speaking, but she watched the way his lips formed the words and missed their meaning. Captivated, she licked her lips. That small movement broke the spell. At once, she knew she'd missed something. "What did you say?"

He gave her a puzzled look, then repeated, "I need to get the Porsche out of the mud." Catherine looked down at their joined hands. She pulled out of his grip easily. When she tried to turn his wounded hand palm up, he resisted at first, then allowed it. Blood oozed from a jagged cut.

"What happened to you?"

"Sliced it on the broken headlight."

"And you've been standing here bleeding the whole time?"

"It's not that bad."

"Why didn't you say something?" Catherine reached for the package of tissues she kept in the console between the front seats. "Here, press a couple of these against the cut."

He shook his head. "Thanks, but they'll just get wet. It's raining, you know." Once again, she experienced his smile, a million volts, hot enough to melt rocks, and any woman's resistance.

He glanced toward the pine trees hugging the roadside. "You wouldn't happen to have a chain saw in the back of your truck, by any chance?"

"Hmm? Oh, no, sorry."

"I was hoping to cut some branches to put under the tires. Without something to give them traction, I don't think the car will make it out of the mud. It's pretty deep."

"How about hay?" she asked. "I've got a whole bale in the back, under the tarp."

"That might work. It's worth a try, anyway."

Catherine started to slide out of the truck's door, thinking she would get out and help, but he blocked her way and said, "I can't get any wetter. There's no sense in you getting soaked, too." He pointed at the flashlight she'd dropped on the passenger seat. "Can I borrow that?"

"Sure."

He shut the door and walked to the back of the truck. She watched him in the side mirror as he reached beneath the tarp and pulled out a huge armful of hay. Then he disappeared in yet another downpour that hid all but the faint, bobbing glow of the flashlight.

Catherine imagined him stuffing hay under the Porsche's wheels and her conscience troubled her. Beset by money worries, and anxious to get home as quickly as she could, she hadn't paid enough attention to her driving. Now, he suffered the consequences of her carelessness, while she sat snug, if not really dry, inside her truck. She hadn't felt so disappointed in herself for months.

The Porsche's taillights flashed. She heard the engine roar. As the car careened from side to side, the single headlight painted brilliant arcs against the falling rain. In the red flare of the car's taillights, she saw mud and hay spewing from beneath the churning wheels. Then the car slid backward and settled into the mire.

The Porsche's lights went out. A minute or so later he was back, tapping at her window. She lowered it enough for him to return the flashlight. "No go," he said. "It'll take a tow truck to pull the car out of that swamp. And that will have to wait until tomorrow."

Catherine felt worse than ever about the accident. "What are you going to do?"

"Walk."

His tone of voice was so matter of fact, and with the noise of the storm, she thought she hadn't heard him quite right. "What did you say?"

He pulled the collar of his coat higher. "I'm going to walk to the nearest town. Without wheels, you walk."

Dismayed at the very idea, she said, "At least go sit in your car, until someone comes along who can help."

"We've been here for a while and haven't seen a single car. It's not likely that anyone will be driving by before morning."

"But..."

"I'm fine. I'll be fine." He turned away and called over his shoulder. "You take care." He was strolling off into the wind and rain in the middle of nowhere. He wasn't fine, he was crazy. Catherine pushed open the truck's door, leaned out, and called after him, "Wait a minute. I'll give you a ride."

Billy stopped, surprised and slightly shocked by her offer. It hadn't occurred to him to ask for a ride, since no sane female alone at night on a deserted road would give him one. She must be crazy, he mused.

He stared at her. She seemed the sort of girl who invited trouble into her life, then generously spread it around. He'd just lived through a couple of weeks of trouble thanks to John and the others, and he didn't want any more. But he was soaking wet and cold and still at least five miles from the nearest café, one he passed earlier as he blasted Carl's shiny black rocket ship the length of Skyline Boulevard. Now, the thought of a burger and fries had his stomach growling. When he considered the weird situations he'd dealt with during the thirty years of his life, he had to admit that most had turned out okay. There didn't seem to be any reason to start second-guessing luck and fate at this point.

"Thanks," he said. "I'd be grateful for a ride."

"Well, get in, then," she said, somewhat un-graciously.

He settled himself inside the truck with his back angled against the passenger door so he could keep an eye on her while she drove. If the truck drifted into oncoming traffic again, he planned to grab the wheel.

Nobody got more than one chance to kill him in a single night.

This time, when she held out the package of tissues, he took some and pressed them against the cut on his hand that still dripped blood. She snapped off the overhead light and started the engine. He reached for his seatbelt and pulled it tight.

By the light of the dashboard display, she looked young, although not as young as Billy had first assumed. On the thin side, with no breasts to speak of, she seemed unfamiliar with the use of makeup. She wore her sandy-blond hair screwed into a knot on top of her head. She swept a stray wisp away from her eyes with one hand, while she concentrated on the looping strip of asphalt rising out of the night in front of the truck's headlights.

Billy held his breath until she put her hand back on the steering wheel.

As the truck gathered speed, she asked, "Where can I take you?"

Before he took Carl's car, Billy intended to cool his anger by walking in the rain. The irony of recent events seemed laughable to him. Still, he had no wish to hurry back to the chaos he'd left behind at the mansion. Better to let everyone calm down, before he tried to talk to them again.

"Without the Porsche, just about anywhere will do," he said with a shrug. "I'm happy to be out of the rain, at least for the time being."

There was something odd about what he'd said and the way he'd said it. Catherine shot him a glance.

"What do you mean, without the Porsche?"

"Just aim for the nearest town, okay?"

Catherine felt uneasy all of a sudden. Maybe her decision to offer him a ride had been a mistake. Her guilt-inspired kindness started to seem less like kindness and more like stupidity. Carefully, she asked, "Is there a problem with the car, other than mud?"

"Sort of."

"Sort of?" The nervous flutter in her stomach became an out-of-control elevator ride to the basement. "You'd better explain."

Billy decided, spur of the moment, to stick to the truth as much as possible, without revealing his identity. The many parts of a pack of lies were always so hard to remember later. He said, "Until about an hour ago I was working at a big estate up the road. One of the guys there lost his temper and tried to mess me up."

"Mess you up?"

"You know, rearrange my face with his fist."

Catherine gasped. "He attacked you?"

"He tried. So I took off before things got totally out of hand."

Catherine nodded. "Good idea," she said.

"Especially since there didn't seem to be an easy way to get past the argument and go back to work. So, when I found the Porsche parked outside, guess you could say I borrowed it." The man smiled, not full blast, merely charming and guileless as a newborn kitten.

Catherine's sympathy for him came to a sudden end. He'd answered the question that had lurked unasked at the back of her mind from the minute she saw him. The question of how a man who dressed like a homeless drifter happened to be driving an expensive sports car. "You stole that car!"

"The owner was kind of ticked off at the time. I don't think he would have loaned it to me willingly."

"Oh my God!" Catherine stared into the rearview mirror. Police cars might be screaming up behind them at any moment. She was helping a car thief escape from the scene of his crime.

That made her an accomplice. What if the police haul me off to jail along with him? "Oh my God!" Catherine said, again.

"Don't panic." The man's smile became a self-satisfied grin. "The car was parked on the far side of the driveway. You can't see much in this rain. I doubt the owner knows his little toy is missing."

"And that makes what you did okay?" Catherine said through clenched teeth, while she tried not to scream at him. Her knuckles were white where her hands gripped the steering wheel.

"It would have, if I could have gotten the damn thing out of the mud and back on the driveway."

Catherine began to calm down. If he could be believed, he hadn't intended to steal the car after all. The situation might not be as bad as she first thought. "If you phone him, maybe he won't press charges."

"Got a phone on you?"

"No." She had left her phone on the bedside table back at the farm, which was not very smart, considering the bad weather and present circumstances. "Don't you have one?"

"Do I look like I carry around expensive electronic devices?" Billy delighted in his impromptu disguise all over again. He was looking forward to telling Carl about it. Billy thought he might keep the baggy coat in case he needed to escape from persistent fans sometime in the future. He stifled a laugh.

Catherine fell silent while she mulled over what she should do. Handsome, charming, loaded with sex appeal, he'd lost his job, and she supposed it would be nearly impossible for him to get another without a recommendation from his current employer. On top of that, he had a distressingly casual attitude about other people's possessions. She was tempted to stop her truck and dump him out on the roadside, storm or no storm, except for one nagging thought: she hadn't been hurt in the accident, while he was sitting beside her bleeding. And no matter how much she wanted to deny the truth, if she hadn't panicked and swerved her truck, neither of them would be in this fix.

Without the Porsche, he couldn't go back to the estate where he'd been working. Judging by his worn clothing, especially his ill-fitting coat, Catherine was sure that he couldn't afford a hotel room. The moment she dropped him off at the nearest town, he'd be just another homeless man searching for shelter. Shelter that might not exist this late in the evening. That left only one thing she could do to make amends.

"My name is Catherine O'Shea," she said.

His full name was William Raven Caldwell, Billy Raven to his friends and fans. He nodded and fed her another truthful lie. "William Caldwell. Billy to my friends."

"Well, Billy," she said, glancing at him, "I can offer you a bed for tonight, if you'd like." His face was unreadable, save for one black brow that arched in skepticism. Catherine said, "No, really, I mean it."

"In that case, thanks."

"Don't thank me yet. The minute we get to my place, you are going to call the owner of that car and tell him where to find it. I am so not going to jail along with you."

Two

Billy eyed the heavy, black hose coiled on the water-stained cement floor and said, "You've got to be kidding."

Catherine smiled. "The shower works like any other, it's just not very fancy."

"Fancy? You mean fancy like inside a room with four walls?"

Catherine laughed. "What are you, some kind of wuss? I use this shower every day." They stood in the central corridor of the shadowy barn looking at an area surrounded on three sides by cement block walls. The narrow space looked very much like a one-car garage. Billy had just discovered that Catherine's apartment attached to the barn had no real bathroom, just a room the size of a closet with a toilet and basin. Showers were taken in a drafty open area designed for washing horses. Billy felt relieved that he wasn't going to be hosed off like a muddy horse.

A shower head jutted from one of the brick walls. The only amenities, and Billy nearly balked at thinking of them as amenities, were a platform constructed of rough wooden slats raised above the cement floor, a yellow plastic shower curtain dangling from a circular rod, and a towel hanging from a hook screwed into the bottom of a shelf stocked with horse shampoo and mane conditioner.

Moving the shower curtain aside, he inspected the wooden platform. "What keeps you from getting splinters in your feet? That looks like a forklift pallet."

Sounding offended, Catherine replied, "My friend at the hardware store said I could have it. I believe in recycling."

Billy smiled at the defiant tilt of her chin as he removed his muddy shoes and socks and stepped onto the rickety platform. He pulled the shower curtain shut to make a private space the size and approximate temperature of a small refrigerator. Then he stripped and handed his soggy clothing out to Catherine. The yellow plastic curtain hid his naked body and his huge grin. He hadn't been so entertained in years. It almost made up for the goose bumps that swarmed over his skin while he waited for the water to run hot.

Alone in her one-room apartment, Catherine changed into dry jeans. She added her wet jeans to Billy's muddy clothes and carried the bundle out to the back porch where she shoved it into her washing machine. While every stitch her guest had been wearing began to slosh through the wash cycle, she folded a blanket over her arm, grabbed a clean towel, and took both into the barn.

Catherine stifled an urge to laugh as she dropped the blanket and towel onto a bale of hay near the shower. Women were supposed to be the weaker sex, always wishing for someone to rescue them. Men were supposed to be fearless and stoic in the face of adversity, like having to shower in a barn. Men didn't complain, they toughed it out. Catherine shook her head at another myth shattered by the lack of traditional plumbing.

Catherine was used to showering in the open. Actually, a shower at the end of each day's work had become an oddly pleasant reminder of the weeks she had spent to make the barn fit for use. She had swept away huge piles of rotting hay and billowing curtains of cobwebs only to face more challenges like the rusty nails that stuck out of the wooden walls practically everywhere she looked. Not to mention several hair-raising hours spent ridding the place of small, scurrying, and long, slithering creatures. But before facing snakes and rats, her most anxious moments had been those spent as she informed her famous, mystery writer mother that she would no longer be working as her personal assistant.

Throughout that encounter, Catherine thought her trembling legs might collapse beneath her while she faced her mother's rage. It had been a mistake to share the details of her plan to start a horse training business. Her mother criticized every point with ruthless mockery. Catherine knew better than to argue when her mother was in the mood to dominate. Finally, she said, "I'll keep in touch." Then she turned and hurried away.

During the weeks that followed, Catherine scouted the foothills of the San Francisco Peninsula, searching for three or four acres of land that she could afford to lease. Time passed without success. She had just promised herself to keep looking no matter how long it might take, when the sign beside a rusted iron gate caught her eye. She brought her truck to a skidding stop. Inches from the truck's front bumper the faded sign included a phone number.

The name of the place was worked into the gate's rusted wrought iron. Beyond the gate, a weed-choked lane curved among gently rising meadows toward an abandoned house. Weathered boards covered several broken windows. Soot stains and charred siding marked the path of the smoke and flames that had ruined the house and left it deserted.

What once had been a charming Elizabethan-style home now stood in the midst of its neglected garden and looked very much like a picture on the cover of a Gothic novel. All that was needed to complete the picture was a young woman in a flowing white dress fleeing in terror across the meadow.

Catherine wasn't worried about the condition of the house. She was very interested in the barn located halfway up the driveway. She pulled a pencil and paper from among the odds and ends that littered the truck's passenger seat and wrote down the phone number printed on the sign.

After speaking to the elderly owner of the property, Catherine inspected the barn. At one end of the building, a large storage room caught her imagination. Piled three feet high with trash and layered with dirt and dust, the room seemed big enough to turn into a small studio apartment. The presence of a small separate space equipped with a toilet and tiny basin was a bonus. She knew the project would require massive amounts of work. Still, she stood in the dim light falling from the grimy windows, determined and undaunted. Two days later, Hidden Lake Farm became Catherine's new home.

Then she watched the amount of money in her savings account shrink with alarming speed. Work that had to pass county building codes required professionals. She hired a cabinet maker to build the kitchen counter and cupboards, an electrician to wire outlets for appliances, and a plumber to install the kitchen sink and the washer and dryer stacked under the eaves on the covered porch outside the back door. She struggled through the rest of the renovations herself, learning do-it-yourself skills as she went along.

When the work was finished and the tiny apartment was move-in ready, the effort and expense turned out to be worth every hour, every sore muscle, and every cent. She had painted the battered walls pale yellow, a sunny summer shade that was cheerful even on a rainy night like this one in early February. She had hidden the splintered wooden floor under peel-and-stick vinyl tiles topped by a pair of colorful rag rugs she purchased at a weekend flea market. Opposite the kitchen area, an armoire stood beside a brass bed covered with a handmade quilt, all of them housewarming gifts from her older brother. Overhead, the high peaked roof and roughhewn rafters of the old barn gave the room a feeling of timelessness.

Catherine turned in a slow circle, trying to see her home as Billy would see it. She ended her inspection with a satisfied smile. He would find nothing to complain about. Recalling his reaction to her shower, she chuckled as she took plates and glasses from the kitchen cupboard and began to set the table for their supper.

A few minutes later, Billy stepped through the doorway leading from the barn into her apartment. Wrapped head to toe in a blanket decorated with pink roses and tiny blue violets, he said, "Thanks for the blanket. Fits perfectly."

Catherine smiled. "Glad I had one in your size. Won't you sit down?" She nodded toward the table.

Billy settled onto one of a pair of ladder-back chairs, propped his arms on the table's well-worn surface, and allowed the ridiculous blanket to pool around his waist. Catherine stood very still and stared.

Stripped of his baggy coat and muddy clothing, he looked nothing like the man who had climbed into her truck. The lamp hanging above the dining table defined in light and shadow every line of his body. Her dazzled eyes traced the width of his muscular shoulders, then lowered to his chest, which looked as finely sculpted as a work of art.

He had finger-combed his hair away from his face. It hung, clean and glinting with blue-black highlights to his shoulder blades. The dark whiskers that shadowed his jaw did little to soften the tough angularity of the face itself. Even as he relaxed, his face still held that hint of menace she had recognized on the rain-swept mountain road. But his eyes were alight with interest as he surveyed her apartment, and his lips were curved again in an appealing smile. Something in Catherine wondered what he would do if she slid her hands across his bare skin.

Aware that her imagination had just soared over a higher fence than she would ever dare to jump on horseback, she spun away. The man was a stranger, out of work, without any immediate prospects, and only one phone call short of facing arrest as a car thief. Despite Billy's vast sex appeal, those facts made her response to him completely wrong, not to mention stupid.

She ducked her head and yanked open the drawer under the kitchen counter that held first aid supplies. An assortment of cosmetics, relics from her former job as her mother's assistant, lay in a jumble at the back of the drawer. She gazed at the stylish containers and wondered why she hadn't thrown them out months ago. She had no need of lip gloss, blush and eyeliner, now. She really should get rid of them.

Frowning, she reached into the drawer and gathered the things she needed to bandage Billy's hand. She avoided looking at him as she dropped a package of gauze, a roll of tape, a bottle of disinfectant, and a pair of scissors on the table.

"Do you want something for pain?" She asked, as she turned back to the open drawer.

"Not necessary."

Billy watched Catherine. Accustomed to female fans chasing after him, it had taken him a while to realize that Catherine's interested inspection of his mostly naked body had flustered her. When he let the blanket drop, she had turned all rosy. Then she did an about-face and stood staring into an open drawer as if it were a portal to another planet, where she'd just discovered little green men. Finally, she slapped some things down on the table without once looking at him. Billy thought Catherine was more entertaining than a busload of back-up singers.

He grinned as he imagined what she might do if he were to pull the blanket from around his waist and toss it over his chair, then take her in his arms and kiss her senseless. Purely as an experiment in human behavior, he assured himself. The idea tantalized. Fantasies did that. That's what made them fantasies in the first place. Sane people didn't act on them. Billy's common sense, and the persistent throbbing in his injured hand, stopped him.

He reached across the table and picked up a small brown bottle that was missing its label. "What's this?"

Catherine couldn't put the moment off. Good manners demanded that she talk to him. She turned and quickly glanced at him. To her great relief, his expression wasn't knowing, or slyly mocking. He wasn't even looking at her. He had opened the little bottle she'd placed on the table, and was holding it under his nose while he sniffed the contents. His nose wrinkled at the sharp smell. The bottom of the bottle thumped the table as he quickly put it back.

"It's disinfectant," she said. "Your hands were covered in mud. There's no telling how many kinds of bacteria got into that cut."

Her no-nonsense tone and the stuff's acrid smell warned him. "Revenge for my high speed driving?"

She smiled just a little and said, "I'm a great believer in natural consequences."

At the sink, she filled a shallow pan with warm water, then set the pan and a clean cloth on the table.

He watched her tip antiseptic into the pan. "I don't think I like the sound of that."

"Would you like a bullet to bite on?" she inquired sweetly.

He laughed, then bit back a hiss of pain and clenched his teeth against the fiery sting as she pushed his hand down into the murky liquid.

He suffered several minutes of torture before she said, "Okay, that should do it."

Once he had dried his hand on the cloth, the fire burned itself out. He sank back into his chair, at ease and still feeling amused.

Then she took him by surprise, asking, "What happened when you called the owner of the Porsche?"

He'd been so relieved that she was busy out in the barn while he phoned Carl, it hadn't occurred to him that she might ask about it later. Now, he scrambled for a truthful, but evasive answer to her question. He shrugged and said, "I found out how many bad words he knows."

"He must have been pretty angry." She began cutting long strips from the roll of gauze.

"You could say that. I won't be going back there any time soon."

"Still, he must want the name of my insurance company. You should call him back and give him the policy number."

Billy held his hand out so she could wrap the gauze around his palm. "I didn't mention you. I told him I overestimated the off-road abilities of his car and mired it in some mud."

"You didn't tell him about the accident?" Catherine's mouth fell open.

"He might have been miffed." He offered this outrageous explanation with such an engaging grin, Catherine couldn't help herself and grinned, too.

"Define miffed," she said.

"More swearing, but in French and German. He spent a couple of years in Europe with the military."

Catherine secured the gauze with several pieces of white tape. "Being the target of a large off-color vocabulary doesn't sound too bad."

"Not bad at all, considering the alternative."

"Strangling you?" she asked, mildly. "The idea crossed my mind recently."

"Very likely." He examined the bandage and grinned. "That was his favorite Porsche."

"He has more than one?"

Billy nodded. "Six, at last count."

"Oh."

Catherine eyed the box of pasta somewhat doubtfully. She hadn't given a moment's thought to the contents of her refrigerator when she'd invited Billy to stay the night. Nor had she considered the hazards of cooking a meal for a half-naked man after she'd shoved every stitch of his clothing into her washing machine. Space in her apartment, which had always been more than adequate for her needs, had shrunk to the intimate size of an average bedroom.

As Catherine eased behind his chair to take a salad bowl from the cupboard, her elbow brushed his shoulder. She gasped at the contact. To her dismay, the fragrance of the soap he had used during his shower, the bargain brand that she used every day, suddenly seemed enticing and erotic. The old saying, 'look but don't touch,' needed to be lengthened to: 'Don't you dare touch him and try very hard not to look.' No matter where she stood in her apartment, she found herself standing much too close to him.

She was determined to avoid noticing his nudity, or how the light falling from the lamp emphasized the sensuous flow of flesh over bone, or how his long hair was drying with a hint of curl at the ends. Her hands shook as she set the salad bowl on the table.

Things were not improved when the washer finished its spin cycle and fell silent. Billy rose from the table to put his clothes in the dryer. Catherine's efforts to cook supper ended as she stood, spoon in hand, and recalled the way his spine curved as it dipped beneath the blanket wrapped around his hips.

"Nuts!" she swore, as the rumble of the dryer brought her to her senses, and she realized that tomato sauce was dripping from her spoon onto the floor. Catherine shook her head. How dumb does a person have to be to stand gawking at empty air?

By the time Billy returned to his seat at the table, she was taking one final swipe with a wet sponge at the red splotches on the floor. Drawing on social skills she had often found useful as well as necessary as her mother's assistant, she smoothed her face into calmer lines. "The pasta will be ready to eat in a couple of minutes."

Catherine toyed with her food. Something peculiar had happened to her mind. She blushed and stammered and acted like an adolescent idiot. She didn't recognize herself. In her previous life, trailing after her famous mother, she'd met plenty of handsome men. None of them had confused her the way Billy did. She kept her eyes focused on her plate of spaghetti.

Billy finished half his pasta before he broke the silence that had followed Catherine to the table. She seemed uneasy, and avoided every opportunity to look at him, which was amazing, since he was sitting directly across from her. Billy sighed and considered that women were sometimes a delightful mystery, and sometimes they were just plain mystifying. No question about it, Catherine O'Shea belonged in the second category.

"Nice place you have here," Billy said, breaking the silence at last.

She raised her eyes in a quick glance and gave him a slight smile. "Thank you."

"I'm curious," he said, setting his fork aside. "Why are you living here in the barn when there is a house just up the driveway?"

"There was a fire. The back half of the house is badly damaged."

Billy turned and looked at Catherine's few belongings. "Is this all you have left?"

"No, no!" She shook her head. "The house burned long before I got here. The place has been deserted for years. That's how I could afford the rent."

She fascinated him. He knew hundreds of women, and not one of them would be caught dead living down the hall from a herd of horses. "So, you haven't been here all that long?"

"About eight months. It took me quite a while to clean out the barn. It was filled with trash and rats." She shuddered at the memory.

"What exactly is it that you do here?" Billy picked up his fork and continued eating.

Catherine watched as he wound long strands of spaghetti around his fork, then lifted the neat bundle to his parted lips. She stopped herself from wondering what his lips would taste like, and picked up her own fork.

"I train Thoroughbreds as show jumpers. Some of them come straight off the racetrack. Not fast enough, you know."

"You take the losers? Isn't that asking for trouble?"

"Not at all. Thoroughbreds are great athletes. With the right training, they can win in the show ring."

"And what happens if the horse has four left feet?"

Catherine chuckled at his description of an uncoordinated horse. "In that case, I train the horse for pleasure riding and make sure it goes to a good home." She pushed the salad bowl toward his plate since he seemed ready for a second helping.

"Thanks." He served himself a small mountain of greens and poured a generous stream of her homemade oil and vinegar dressing on top. "It sounds like you've been working with horses for a long time, but you said you've only been in business for a few months."

"That's right. Actually, I got started as a teenager, working for a professional trainer. I've kept at it in my free time ever since."

"Did you grow up on a ranch?"

"Far from it." Catherine reached for a piece of garlic bread. "I grew up in San Francisco, in a family of artists and writers. Fans followed us everywhere, most of them wanted my mother's autograph. It was impossible to leave our house without being stopped by someone."

Billy sympathized. He'd learned that fame had a down side. Pushy fans were only a small part of it. Handling the business and legal demands of his music career had turned out to be frustrating, more often than not. And especially frustrating when your best friends let you down, like they had over the last couple of weeks. He asked, "Would I know who your parents are?"

"Probably." Catherine shifted uneasily in her chair. His background had to be so different from hers, she was afraid he might think she was boasting. Still, she knew it would be rude not to explain. "My mother's last novel became a hit movie. Everyone saw it."

When she mentioned the title, *Death Stalkers*, Billy's eyebrows rose in surprise. "What about your father? You said you grew up surrounded by artists and writers."

"My father paints portraits of famous people and landscapes of historic places. He owns a gallery in San Francisco and another in New York."

Billy had been to her father's New York gallery. His paintings of Venice were amazing. Billy kept his expression bland, with just the right touch of polite interest.

"What about brothers and sisters?" He asked the question already knowing the answer.

"Just one brother. One is quite enough." Catherine laughed. "He's five years older and even more famous than my parents."

"Sinjin O'Shea." Billy watched Catherine's face as he spoke her brother's name.

A fond smile curved her lips. "Yes. The Golden Boy. How did you guess?"

Two years earlier, Billy had met Catherine's brother at one of Cherokee's concerts. A stunning blonde with a backstage pass introduced them. Billy remembered him as a man whose eyes missed nothing and who seemed amused at the blonde's attempts to impress him.

Billy avoided Catherine's question by asking one of his own. "The Golden Boy?"

"Sin was eleven years old when he published his first children's book, *Quacking Up Duck*. By the time he turned sixteen, his picture books were outselling Sendak."

"And you resented him?"

"No, not really. I adored him and felt jealous of him, all at the same time." She looked thoughtful for a moment. "Mostly, I idolized him."

"What about now?"

"We're best friends. Last week Sin dropped by to

do some sketches. He still likes ducks after all these years, and Hidden Lake has dozens."

Billy hoped Catherine's brother had painted a portrait of every damned one of those ducks already, and didn't need to paint another. Running into O'Shea again would wreck Billy's plans. He'd been thinking of ways to extend his stay on the farm. Catherine didn't have a clue to his identity. He wanted to keep it that way. He enjoyed talking with her. He felt more relaxed this evening than he had in years. If she discovered that poor Billy Caldwell, unemployed car borrower, was more famous than her whole family put together, the peaceful interlude would end, and she'd be mad as hell.

His way of life included everything she'd gotten away from. Hordes of fans surrounded him wherever he went, demanding autographs and taking selfies. Members of the entertainment press hounded him for exclusive interviews. Ever-present photographers jumped out of the bushes beside his driveway, snapping candid photos of anyone who arrived at his home. Then there were the women who wanted whatever they could get, getting too close too soon to be trusted. He'd learned that lesson early in his career.

Catherine didn't look at him with calculation in her eyes. She came from a sophisticated family, but seemed to be untouched by the temptations of their world. She seemed honest and generous and hard working. And impetuous, when he thought about the fact that she had invited a stranger into her home.

He let his eyes travel over her slim figure. She stood with her back to him, up to her elbows in soapy water, scrubbing the pasta pan. After their arrival at the farm, she hadn't taken the time to fix her hair. Sandy colored curls tumbled out of the loosened knot on top of her head. Every so often, she brushed them away from her face with the back of a wet hand. He could see the slight jut of her breast against her shirt as she lifted the pan out of the sink and placed it in the dish drainer to dry. He sat close enough to touch her, watching her and thinking about her body, while she remained unaware of him.

Billy thought her careless attitude toward his presence was ample proof that she could use a friend to protect her from predatory males. It was a good thing he wasn't one of them. She had nothing in common with the women he dated. That meant he could enjoy her company without any of the usual complications. As her friend, he could keep a watchful eye on her. All he had to do was figure out a way to stick around for a few days.

Catherine rinsed out the sink and paused to dry her hands on a dishtowel. "That's the last of the dishes. Let's get you settled for the night." She reached into the cupboard under the sink and pulled out a box of super-size trash bags.

They made their way to the abandoned house in the pouring rain. Catherine wore a yellow slicker. Over clothes still warm from the dryer, Billy sported hooded rain gear constructed from black plastic bags and packing tape. Catherine didn't own an umbrella, but made up for its lack with her own kind of cockeyed creativity. He felt particularly grateful that he hadn't been forced to wear Carl's jacket, now dripping from a hanger onto the floor of the barn. He'd wanted very much to avoid the cold clutches of that coat. Enough to let Catherine wrap him up in plastic like a mummy from the top of his head to well below his knees. And now, his hands were trapped uselessly at his sides and he couldn't take a step longer than six inches without tripping. He hunched his shoulders, bowed his head beneath the heavy rain, and shivered each time icy drops slid down the back of his neck where a piece of tape had pulled loose.

Catherine's flashlight led the way, bobbing along a rough path. He stumbled after her, feeling awkward and ridiculous. The ruined house loomed as a darker shadow against the night sky. He could just make out a flight of shallow steps rising between the heavy pillars of a wide porch. As they climbed the steps, the flashlight's beam reflected in a blaze of diamonds from leaded glass windows on either side of the front door. At the far end of the porch, a wooden swing rocked on creaking chains as the storm winds gusted around it.

Catherine planted her feet and leaned her shoulder against the massive redwood door. She shoved and the door opened with a loud grating sound just wide enough to let them slide through sideways. She pushed the hood of her slicker back and said, "Welcome to Hidden Lake Farm Bed and Breakfast." She swept her flashlight around the foyer and added, "It's pretty spooky with no electricity."

Glancing around, Billy had to agree. To his right, a doorway draped in cobwebs opened into a room filled with bulky shapes covered with ghostly white sheets. He felt as if he'd stepped onto the set of a low budget horror flick. He half expected to see an actor dripping fake blood leap from behind the shrouded furniture. Maybe not so fake, he thought suddenly, and maybe not an actor. Catherine had told him that her elderly landlady's husband had died in the fire. Billy stared into the dead man's parlor, scarcely breathing, waiting to see if anything in the darkened room moved, or made creepy sounds.

Another stray drop of cold water slid down the back of his neck and broke the grip of his overactive imagination. Embarrassed by his own silliness, Billy struggled out of his rain gear and looked for a place to put it.

Catherine said, "I'll take that." She tossed the soggy mass out onto the porch, then forced the front door shut. She turned to him and said, "There's a room on the second floor where you can sleep."

She trained her flashlight onto the broad staircase that curved upward, enclosing the foyer on three sides. Billy gazed up the stairs to the point where the light faded and darkness blocked the way. He asked, "Why has the house been abandoned like this?"

"After her husband died, Maude couldn't bear to live here. But she couldn't part with the house either."

"So the whole place was deserted, until you rented it?"

"Without major repairs, no one had any use for

the house. Except for my brother. Follow me and I'll show you the artist's lair."

Billy trailed after Catherine as she jogged up the stairs. Halfway up, he stopped to listen to the sounds of the storm. Somewhere on the floor above a loose shutter caught by the wind banged a furious drumbeat against the side of the house. Behind him, a swinging tree branch scraped across a window. Billy imagined fingernails clawing the inside of a coffin lid. The hairs on the back of his neck rose. He sprinted up the stairs toward the room where pale light fell from the open door into the pitch black hallway.

Catherine was busy lighting candles. Three glowed in silver candlesticks among a jumble of art supplies strewn on a long table angled against the paint-splattered easel in the center of the room. Directly overhead, the falling rain clattered like Spanish castanets on a wide skylight. As Billy watched, Catherine placed a fourth candle on top of a chest of drawers in the far corner. She switched off her flashlight and said, "Sin chose this room because of the skylight."

Billy dropped a hand on the cluttered table. "Is this your brother's furniture?"

"Only the easel. The rest came from other rooms near the front of the house. The things in here smelled very smoky."

"Some of this looks valuable," he said, touching one of the silver candlesticks. "Are you sure it's okay for me to use this room?"

"It won't be a problem, as long as Sin doesn't show up unexpectedly." She tipped her head back and looked up at the rain pelting the skylight. "Which is close to impossible in this weather."

"What about your landlady?"

"She said Sin could use the room as long as he wanted. Maude fell madly in love with my brother the moment she met him." Catherine rolled her eyes. "When he's being charming, he bewitches women. Of all ages, it seems."

"Another of his talents?" Billy grinned at her disgruntled expression.

"Like whipped cream on a perfect slice of chocolate mousse pie."

Billy laughed, then became serious once more. "I'm not your brother."

Catherine was well aware of that fact. Her eyes met his, then darted away. She said, "I'm positive neither Maude nor my brother will mind if you sleep here tonight. Consider yourself a temporary guest."

He nodded. "Okay. I won't take advantage of your hospitality."

Catherine studied his face for a moment. She understood that he meant she would be safe in his company. It wasn't something she needed to hear. Long before she rose from the dinner table and cleared away their dirty dishes, she was sure he wouldn't harm her. Not physically, anyway. But emotional harm? That was another question entirely, while she struggled every moment to hide her crazy attraction to him. She assured him, "I'm not worried about that."

She put just enough emphasis on her last two words to make Billy's eyebrows arch in expectation. "You're worried about something else?"

"No, not a thing! What could possibly worry me?"

Billy could think of plenty of reasons for a woman to worry about inviting a stranger into her home. He made a little clucking noise, a disdainful sound. "Very little seems to worry you."

Catherine bristled at his tone. "You think I'm irresponsible."

He shook his head. "Not after finding out how much effort you've put into restoring the barn and starting your business."

That sounded like praise to Catherine, until he went further.

"I'd say you're a bit too impulsive." His smile was engaging. "Actually, you're a lot too impulsive."

No charming smile could soothe the sting of his criticism. Catherine caught her breath before she blurted out one of the furious words crowding the tip of her tongue. She wanted to say: If it hadn't been for my so-called impulsive actions, you'd still be walking down a rain-drenched mountain road in the dark, not standing in front of me, well fed and dry, and wearing a smug expression.

She couldn't remember when she'd been so angry. What an arrogant, ungrateful jerk! Too bad they weren't back in her truck. She'd be tempted to kick him out onto the roadside, then run over him.

"First impressions are always so reliable when judging a person's character," she snarled. "You know next to nothing about me. And that's how I plan to keep it."

She stalked over to the antique day bed set against one wall and yanked a rolled sleeping bag from beneath it.

Billy watched in amusement as Catherine slammed the sleeping bag down on the narrow bed. Temper tinted her cheeks and added fire to her eyes. The blushing innocent he'd taken her for had disappeared. In her place stood a fair-haired Valkyrie in blue jeans and boots who looked mad enough to run him through with her sword, if she'd had one. Instead, she stomped to the door, paused just long enough to stab him with a killing look, and pointed to the bathroom across the hall. Rather than wishing him a good night, she said, "There's no hot water, but the toilet works."

Catherine's anger still smoldered as she got ready for bed. She fumed as she arranged her pillows by punching them flat instead of fluffing them into airy clouds to cushion her head. She snapped off the bedside lamp, pulled the covers up to her chin, and stared unseeing into the dark space beyond the rafters, while the whole ugly scene in the studio replayed in her mind. The man was a complete jerk. She'd rid herself of his unwelcome presence in the morning, at daybreak, or even earlier. Maybe she'd haul him out of the old house still zipped in her brother's sleeping bag.

She imagined William Caldwell, Billy to his friends, though she doubted that such an imbecile had any friends, complaining loudly as she dragged him down each uncarpeted step of the long, curving staircase. Catherine wore a satisfied smile as she rolled onto her side and let herself drift into sleep.

Three

Catherine woke tangled in her blankets. She kicked free of the sheet that trapped one ankle and sighed. Her dreams of Billy had been vivid, every detail the X-rated handiwork of her own imagination. She cringed at the memory.

She squinted at her clock and groaned. She'd slept late. Last night, too furious to follow her usual routine, she'd forgotten to set the alarm. The clock sat silent and accusing on the bedside table, more proof that bringing Billy to the farm was beyond foolish. Disgusted with herself, she swung her legs over the side of the bed and plodded barefoot across the room to start the coffee maker.

While the coffee brewed, Catherine showered and dressed in jeans and a flannel shirt. She tugged a comb through the tangles in her hair and hid the hopeless result under a red bandana. She stepped out onto the porch. Her boots were muddy and frozen. She had dropped them there last night after leaving Billy at the abandoned house. Thinking of him, she knocked the mud from her boots with more force than necessary and jammed her feet into the stiff leather. Then she scurried back to the warmth of her apartment and poured herself a mug of steaming black coffee.

The aroma alone was enough to pry her eyes wide open. She caught a glimpse of herself in the mirror that hung beside the door and stuck out her tongue. She laughed. The woman in the mirror returned a grin and looked very much as if she expected to enjoy the day. Or at least the part of the day that was left after she got rid of Billy.

Catherine juggled her mug of coffee out of one hand and into the other as she pulled on her jacket and stepped onto the porch once more. The crisp scent of pine drifted across the meadow from the grove that hid Hidden Lake. Birds, early risers long awake, sang their separate songs among the trees. The rain had gone, and it seemed that her vexing guest was still asleep in the house on the opposite side of the barn. "Out of sight, out of mind," she said, and decided to deal with him after she finished feeding the horses. The irritation she felt at the idea of having to confront Billy faded away, and the tension in her shoulders eased.

Catherine admired the clear blue of the morning sky for a few minutes, then set her empty mug on the porch and bounded out into the stable yard. Skirting the worst of the ice-crusted puddles, she jogged to her truck and unhitched the trailer. Then she opened the pickup's storage box and lugged out the waterproof blanket that belonged to her newest student. The colt would need the heavy blanket outdoors during the afternoon. Inside the barn, she draped the blanket over a sawhorse near the young Thoroughbred's stall.

Catherine could hear the colt moving restlessly inside the stall. A more docile animal might have poked his head over the half door to watch her while she began her morning chores. Not this particular horse. He shuffled through the deep straw and pawed the floor to show his discontent.

Catherine shrugged. This seemed as good a time as any to begin to make friends with him. She opened the stall door and slipped inside. In a soft tone she called to him, "How are you doing this morning, Lucky?" She'd chosen that nickname for him because he was lucky to be in one piece after last night's almost accident.

When the colt turned to face her, she smiled. At least he hadn't shown her his heels. Maybe he'd done enough kicking while he rode in her trailer last night. She fished in her jacket pocket for one of the ever-present chunks of raw carrot she carried. Still talking softly, she offered the treat. He took a step toward her and she held the carrot out to him on the palm of her hand. He swept it into his mouth, crunching and gulping it down. Then he sniffed her jacket pockets, searching for more. "You're not so tough," she told him, and offered him another piece of carrot.

Catherine bent and ran her fingers over the colt's legs, reassuring herself again that he hadn't been injured when she brought her truck to such a sudden stop. Satisfied, she took a hoof pick from the back pocket of her jeans and cleaned his hooves. She gave Lucky a friendly slap on his haunch and carried his food bucket out of the stall to refill it. When she returned, she cleaned bits of hay out of his water basin. Finished, she closed him in his stall and went to feed the other horses in her stable.

As the horses ate their way toward the bottoms of buckets heaped with alfalfa cubes, Catherine stood in the center aisle of the barn and watched dust motes drift in the shaft of sunlight falling from a high window. At this time of day, the barn felt especially peaceful. In the calming quiet, all her troubles seemed to slip away. She let her thoughts drift. When she realized that her thoughts had drifted over to the old house and to Billy, she forced herself to think of something else, something like what she wanted for breakfast.

Her morning routine always gave her a hearty appetite, and breakfast was the one meal where she indulged herself. Lunch was usually a carton of yogurt and chunks of raw vegetables, some of which she shared with the horses. By sundown, more tired than hungry, she heated a bowl of soup, or made a sandwich to eat while she watched television, before falling exhausted into bed.

Catherine walked down the corridor toward the door to her apartment. Today she'd make biscuits, with crisp bacon and freshly squeezed orange juice. She had enough oranges, but she would have to drive to the market in town for a pound of bacon and a box of baking mix. The meal she had in mind would be worth the trip. Besides, she needed to stock up on food after feeding Billy last night.

She sighed. The problem with offering shelter from the storm to a sexy car thief was how to get rid of him the next day. Determined to send him on his way, she thought she ought to feed him first. Afterward, she wouldn't owe him anything more. She added a dozen eggs to her shopping list and hurried out to her truck.

A ray of cool, winter sunshine fell across Billy's face from the studio's skylight. He opened his eyes to a brilliant blue sky and what felt like morning in the Arctic. His breath formed a puffy white cloud a few inches above his nose. Curious to see if his face had frozen during the night, he slid one hand out of the sleeping bag and rubbed his stubbled cheek. He could still feel his fingers touching his face. He smiled. He'd heard that Alaskan hunters constructed houses out of ice. If they could stand it, he could stand it. He unzipped the sleeping bag and sat up, then yelped as the cold air gripped him.

His jeans and shirt lay on the floor. He scooped them up and dived back inside the warm sleeping bag. He wrestled into his shirt and buttoned it all the way to his chin. He jerked his jeans up his legs and under his hips. Knowing he'd have to stand to fasten the button-fly, Billy swore, then climbed out of the sleeping bag. Shivering, he buttoned his jeans. Then he rammed his feet into his muddy shoes. If anything, his shoes were colder than the bare wooden floor they had been sitting on. He decided that the next time he crashed a car in the dead of winter he'd make sure he was wearing wool socks.

He flexed his injured hand. The pain was almost gone, but he decided to leave the bandage in place. He blew on his hands to warm them and watched the color of his fingertips turn from bluish white to a healthier shade. Hunching his shoulders against the chill air, he rolled the sleeping bag and stowed it under the bed.

The room by daylight didn't seem the same. Last night, his imagination had run wild, so wild he'd let the candles burn down in their holders as he lay listening to the old house creak and moan in the storm winds. All appeared tranquil now in the morning, tranquil and very cold.

The worktable in the middle of the room held brushes and tubes of paint, and a bunch of other stuff he didn't recognize. Billy wondered if Catherine's brother might have left anything more useful. Like a goose down parka. He doubted it. Still, he opened the dresser drawers one after another.

In the bottom drawer he found two paint-smeared sweatshirts jammed among a pile of rags. Billy held one of the sweatshirts up by the shoulder seams to check the size. It would do with a little stretching. The second sweatshirt seemed larger. He tugged them on, one atop the other, before he walked down to the barn to see if Carl's jacket had dried overnight.

Catherine drove past the barn without stopping to unload the groceries. At the top of the driveway, her truck plowed through the neglected yard and mowed down a row of long-dead rosebushes. There was a hole in the house where the front door should have been. The missing door lay across a pair of wooden kegs set on the brown remnants of the lawn. Billy leaned over the door, slashing strips of wood from one edge. The only notice he took of her arrival was a quick glance over his shoulder, as her truck stopped on the lawn a few yards behind him.

Catherine shoved her way out of her truck and marched through the carpet of wooden curls drifting in the breeze. The pungent odor of wounded redwood filled her nose.

"What the heck do you think you're doing?" she demanded.

"Good morning," he said, looking at her at last.

Catherine stood stiff-backed, with her hands on her hips and a frown on her face. Her voice was as frigid as a Viking fjord. The Valkyrie from the night before had gotten up on the wrong side of her bed. Billy put the carpenter's plane down on top of the door and waited.

First thing that morning, he had hurried down to the barn, hoping Carl's coat might have dried overnight. It still drooped, wet and clammy, from its hanger, and made the two sweatshirts he wore seem especially warm and comfortable, and much better than freezing to death. He tapped on Catherine's door. When she didn't answer, he went looking for her and discovered her truck was missing. He jogged back into the barn to get out of the cold wind stirring the meadow grasses.

The building was filled with a spring-like fragrance. The new-mown-lawn smell was unexpected in the middle of winter. Intrigued, he traced the scent to the small green cubes that spilled from a sack propped in the doorway of an unoccupied stall. He'd discovered a horse pantry. In the stall, sacks were piled in a heap that reached above the level of his chest. Labels on some of the sacks told him they were filled with oats. Other sacks held more of the green cubes. He crumbled one of the cubes between his fingers. The strong odor of alfalfa clung to his skin even after he wiped his hands on his jeans.

He realized then that Catherine must have been up for several hours, working in the barn while he slept. He felt guilty as hell for imposing on her. If he hadn't been hiding his identity, he would have hired a limo and checked into a five star hotel in San Francisco, the kind of hotel that kept fans away from the famous. Instead, last night he had removed his wallet from his pocket while he stripped in Catherine's ridiculous shower. After she scurried off to wash his muddy clothes, he had hidden the wallet in an inside pocket of Carl's wet coat. The fact that the coat was still soggy this morning had probably saved him. Catherine would have had no reason to touch the coat beyond testing the hem for wetness, just as he had done. Having found a better hiding place, he pulled a twenty and a couple of fives from his wallet before he tucked it between two bags of oats in the horse pantry.

Billy figured he needed a way to pay for his night's stay and for the food Catherine had served him. Recalling that she nearly broke her shoulder opening the front door at the old house last night, he searched the barn and a nearby shed, and gathered the tools he needed. Then he set to work.

He was almost finished with the job when Catherine came barreling up the driveway in her truck. He figured the speed of her pickup summed up the intensity of her temper.

Now, ignoring her lack of a response to his pleasant greeting, Billy replied to Catherine's angry question. "It's a peace offering after last night's little misunderstanding."

"Misunderstanding?" She looked at the door through narrowed eyes. "Let me get this straight. You're making up for making me angry last night by making me furious this morning?"

"Apparently so."

Billy wiped his hands against the seat of his pants. He offered her the one without the grubby bandage. "Friends?"

She left his hand hanging in space while she ran her fingers across the raw wood of the door. "Where did you get the idea that you should gouge pieces out of this door?"

He stuck his hands in his pockets. "I planed the door, gouging is unprofessional. I've worked construction."

That was truthful, and sketchy, like everything he'd told her in the past twelve hours. The whole truth would have him out on the street faster than a gate crasher at one of his concerts. He'd worked construction, all right, but for his uncle's company in Texas, and only for eight months prior to Cherokee's first album going platinum. Billy hid a grin. Multimillionaires didn't gouge doors, they planed doors for the pleasure of doing something useful with their own two hands.

Catherine gazed at Billy. She knew work in the building industry could be uncertain. Men were hired in good times only to be let go a few months later when home sales slumped. In midwinter, the market for new houses might be poor, making it difficult for Billy to find another job. She remembered he'd said something of the sort last night. Being fired must have been hard to take. Maybe that explained why he seemed so reluctant to talk about himself. At any rate, Billy seemed sure of his skill as a carpenter. If he didn't finish the job, she'd just have to hire someone else to do it.

"Okay," she said, "the house is a wreck anyway, you probably can't do much harm."

Billy smiled at her less than enthusiastic attitude. At least the ice was beginning to thaw.

Catherine asked, "What exactly are you doing?"

"I'm trimming the door to fit the frame. It's much less trouble than taking the frame apart and rebuilding it."

"That makes sense, I guess."

"When I hang the door back on its hinges, it'll open and close slick as grease on a hot griddle." He grinned.

During his exploration of the barn, Billy had discovered quite a few things that needed fixing.

The repairs were mostly simple tasks. He assumed that Catherine intended to do them herself, but had been too busy setting up her business to begin on them. Maybe he could turn an offer of work into an invitation to stick around for a few days.

"Slick as butter on hot biscuits," she corrected him. "By the time you finish here, I'll have your breakfast ready."

Billy hung both sweatshirts on a hook inside the back door and rolled up the sleeves of his shirt before washing his hands at the kitchen sink. Catherine had set the table for two with flatware and glasses, mugs of steaming coffee, a stick of butter on a saucer, a bottle shaped like a little bear full of honey, and a pitcher of orange juice. He chose the same chair he'd taken last night and sat down. She set a plate stacked with eggs and bacon and biscuits before him.

"Don't wait for me," she said, as she broke more eggs into the hot frying pan.

"It seems rude to eat while you cook. But..." He picked up a piece of bacon, crisp, golden brown, and perfect. He bit off half and sighed in satisfaction.

The fresh-squeezed orange juice smelled like perfume and tasted candy-tart in a way the carton stuff never could match. As Billy sipped it, he watched Catherine over the rim of his glass. When she brought her plate to the table and sat down, he said, "This is very good."

Catherine laughed. "You're just hungry. It's been quite a while since supper."

Billy frowned. She'd thrown away the compliment as if it meant nothing to her. "I'm serious. These eggs are first rate and the bacon is crisp, just the way I like it. You could open a restaurant."

She tipped her head toward the door leading into the barn and the horses beyond. "I have a restaurant. Only I serve hay and rolled oats mixed with molasses."

He nodded. "To clients who are notoriously poor tippers."

"Not to mention their table manners."

"Terrible. You'd think they'd all been raised in a barn." He cocked an eyebrow and grinned at her.

"Exactly." She hesitated. He'd been pretty closed mouth about himself up to now. And even though she didn't like to pry, his teasing comment gave her an opening to learn more about him. "What about you? Where were you raised?"

"Austin."

Great, she thought, a one word answer. Finding out anything more might involve a little prying after all.

Thinking he must have gotten his dark, exotic looks from his mother's family, she asked, "Is your mother Hispanic?"

"Native American."

Two words this time. Now what? She took a sip of coffee and decided he might be less reserved if she shared something about herself. "I was in Austin a few summers ago. My mother spoke at a writers' conference."

"Some folks say Texas in summer is about the same temperature as winter in hell."

She chuckled. "You're so right. It was over a hundred degrees every afternoon."

"When it's that hot, most tourists find things to do indoors until dusk. After it cools off, they come out looking for fun and Southern hospitality."

"I noticed that." Though she wouldn't offend him by saying so, she thought Austin would be a great place for vampires. They'd have their pick of potential victims strolling along the streets after dark. The city even listed a colony of bats as a tourist attraction. One evening, she stood in a crowd along the riverside and watched thousands of bats swoop from under a bridge into the moonlit sky. She said, "There are lots of small clubs where you can listen to music."

"Are you into music?" He appeared to be studying her.

She shook her head. "Not me, my brother. Sin asked me to take a photo of the statue of Stevie Ray Vaughn in the park. He was a famous guitar player."

"I know." His grin would have suited a large cat who'd just eaten a neighbor's Chihuahua.

She rolled her eyes. Of course, he'd know of Stevie Ray Vaughn. He grew up in Austin. She felt exasperated. Not just with her own idiotic comment, but with the direction their conversation had taken. They'd ended up talking about the weather and music, neither of which had anything to do with him.

Catherine was frowning again. Her change of mood swept away the last trace of Billy's secret delight that began when she started talking about the music scene in Austin. But that topic had skimmed too close to the truth for comfort, so Billy changed the subject. "I could replace the broken glass in those two windows in the barn."

The look Catherine turned on him was full of speculation. "How much would you charge to do the job?"

"Just my board and room for a few days, if that's okay with you."

"For a couple of windows?"

She sounded unconvinced. He smiled at her and upped his offer. "The barn leaks and there are shingles in the shed. I could patch the roof, too."

Some mad impulse held Catherine in its grip. Billy could infuriate her one minute, then charm her the next. At the moment, he was being friendly and helpful. It drove her crazy. Last night, she had decided to kick him off Hidden Lake Farm without a qualm. This morning, she found him dressed in rags, repairing her absent landlady's front door. All he had to do was flash her a smile and her backbone melted.

She felt more than a little awed that any man could influence her that way, or that easily. And now he'd done it again by offering to do a few odd jobs. She wasn't completely naïve. He wanted a job and a place to stay. She could provide both. In truth, she had a daunting list of things that needed to be done around the farm, repairing the leaky roof, for one. She knew it might be months before she could find the time to do any of them herself. Or earn enough money to hire someone to do them. As long as she and Billy both got what they needed from the arrangement, she supposed he could stay for a few days. She didn't see any harm in it, and she could stretch her budget enough to cover his food and a couple of panes of glass.

"The windows will have to wait, until I have time to pick up new glass at the hardware store," she said. "But it would be great if you could fix the roof before it starts raining again."

"Okay." Patching the roof would take most of the day. He had talked his way into at least one more night sleeping on a narrow bed in an icy room in a creepy abandoned house. He marveled that guaranteed discomfort seemed so appealing.

He pushed his chair back from the table. "I'll get started on the roof right now."

Catherine jumped up. "No, wait." Without thinking, she reached out to stop him. Beneath her grip, where there should have been a shirtsleeve, her fingers found his naked flesh. His skin felt firm and warm. Warm and alive. And dangerous. She jerked her hand back, as if she had been burned.

"Was there something else?" he asked.

His question cut through the sudden rush of desire that had scrambled her brain. She stepped away from him while she tried to remember what she wanted to say. "Something else? Oh, yes!"

Catherine drew a calming breath. "I'm way behind schedule this morning. Could you help me clean the stalls, before you start on the roof?"

"Sure. Just show me what to do." He pulled one of her brother's paint-spattered sweatshirts over his head as he spoke.

Seeing him dressed again in rags reminded her that Billy's way of life seemed to be the exact opposite of hers. He'd as much as said that he drifted from one temporary job to the next, while all of her energies went into building her business and earning the respect of the community of horse owners. He didn't appear to have much energy at all when it came to setting goals and achieving them. He looked gorgeous. He stirred her and filled her head with visions of romance. He was very much like the hero in one of her mother's novels, sexy and shallow. It was foolish to think there could be anything lasting between them. With a sigh, Catherine forced herself to accept the truth, and carried their dirty breakfast dishes to the sink.

A few minutes later, armed with shovels, they worked side by side in an open stall, filling a wheelbarrow with dirty straw. Catherine said, "Once we clean out all the horse poop, I'll show you how to line the stall with fresh straw. Then you can do the next one all by yourself." She grinned at him.

Billy aimed the contents of his shovel toward the wheelbarrow. The pile of horse poop sailed through the dusty air in a low arc and landed on target with a satisfying thump. "I noticed you didn't offer me any lessons in how to shovel this stuff."

She laughed. "Somehow, after listening to your story last night, I felt sure you'd had previous experience."

Billy paused, smiling at her. "Very funny. But I haven't told you one single thing that wasn't true." He'd just left out all of the most important details.

"Right." Her voice was loaded with skepticism. "You've admitted that you lied to the guy who owns the Porsche, which you stole. That certainly makes you trustworthy. Next thing, you'll probably tell me you're Prince Charming and I'm Cinderella and this is a glass slipper." She lifted one foot in a scuffed boot and waggled it in the air.

"Anything is possible," Billy replied, poker-faced.

Catherine said, "I've had enough of fairy tales. I grew up in one." She nodded toward the corridor beyond the open stall door. "This is real. I prefer my present life."

"I can understand that."

She shook her head. "Not if you haven't lived it, you can't. A life of luxury isn't at all what it's cracked up to be, believe me. Everyone wants to be rich, to win the lottery, to hit the jackpot. The winners never talk about the downside of winning."

"Tell me." He leaned his shovel against the wooden wall of the stall.

"Well, the effort it takes to maintain that kind of lifestyle is tremendous. The demands are endless." She looked away and caught her lower lip between her teeth.

Billy wondered what more she might have said, if she hadn't stopped herself. It probably wasn't anything good. As gently as possible, he prompted, "What kind of demands?"

He watched her take a deep breath and let it out before she said, "Travel plans, meetings with editors and book publishers, with gallery owners and auction houses, paying the bills, keeping records of every transaction, scheduling appointments with accountants, with bankers, with critics, with movie producers, you name it."

He studied her, disbelieving. She seemed too young to have taken on that amount of responsibility. "You did all that for your parents?"

"Yes. And I found myself surrounded by social climbers and sycophants. I didn't want to end up so cynical that life lost its ability to astonish me."

"What would it take to astonish you, now?"

She leaned on her shovel, an impish grin teasing the corners of her mouth. "Maybe finding out that you really are Prince Charming."

Billy stepped forward, near enough to crowd her against the wall. "I don't have a glass slipper, but let's see if this fits." He slid one hand behind her neck to draw her close and felt a surge of pleasure as her eyes opened wide in surprise.

Gentle. She hadn't imagined that his kiss would be so gentle. He brushed his lips across hers. Then the tip of his tongue traced the line between her lips, asking her to open for him. On a sigh, Catherine complied. When his arms tightened around her, holding her close, some unused part of her heart began to soar.

The shovel fell from her hands, banging once against the wooden wall, before it scraped its way down to the straw-littered floor. Her hands stroked upward over his encircling arms. She felt his heat rising through the sweatshirt he wore. Her fingers found the strip of leather he'd used to tie back his hair. She pulled it loose and the heavy black mane fell about his face and slid across her cheeks like warm silk.

If it was wrong, if it was unforgivable, if it was breaking a promise he'd made to himself to be her friend and nothing more, holding Catherine in his arms still filled Billy with wonder.

If she had protested, he would have let her go instantly. But she didn't protest. She melted against him and wrapped her arms around his neck. She took his breath away. And she tasted sweet and intoxicating. She went to his head like hundred-year-old brandy. He fought to keep from plundering the mouth she lifted to his.

He let his tongue caress and lightly tease, without alarming her with his sudden greed to take more. He moved his hands over her and resisted the urgent need to rip away the flannel shirt that barred his hands from the warmth of her skin. He touched her cheeks with his fingertips and tilted her head so he could explore her mouth more intimately. Her body strained against his and her breath escaped as a low moan. He heard the sound of her surrender and pulled away before he plunged them into the torrent of passion that rushed like a wild river between them.

Billy felt dazed. He'd kissed Catherine in a lighthearted way, secretly pleased that in real life thousands of women actually did think of him as Prince Charming. First he'd been astonished by Catherine's response, then unbelievably aroused. He needed time to figure out what to do about it. He couldn't become involved with her while he continued to deceive her. Yet the moment he told her the truth, any relationship, romantic or otherwise, would be over before it could begin. Catherine was sure to choose her tranquil existence on the farm over dating someone she'd known for less than twenty-four hours, especially if that someone was world famous and a liar.

Billy straightened. Catherine's arms fell from his shoulders. Although mere inches separated them, it seemed to her that several universes could not fill that space. He'd left her wanting. The shock she felt at her own behavior was just beginning to register, when he let his forehead rest lightly against hers. For long moments they stood motionless in the silence of the old barn.

It took all of Catherine's willpower to keep from fleeing to the farthest, darkest corner of the barn.

What had begun as a simple kiss had left her without defenses. If Billy hadn't stopped when he did, she would have done whatever he asked. She hadn't just humiliated herself, she'd betrayed herself and all that she believed.

I must be out of my mind, she thought, thoroughly unsettled. I never should have acted in such a reckless way.

She had always believed that sexual intimacy ought to be reserved for a committed relationship, not for a ten minute roll in the hay in an empty barn. So I'm old-fashioned, so what? She was probably the only twenty-three-year-old virgin in existence, but that hadn't mattered to her up to now. No man had made her weak with desire, until she kissed Billy Caldwell.

"Catherine?" Her name came as a feather-light breath fanning her lips.

She raised her head, breaking the slight contact between them. Too upset to know what to say to him, she said nothing. She stood looking into his hooded eyes, until shame made her bow her head and look away.

"Catherine, that kiss didn't work."

"What?" Her head came up and she blinked in confusion.

He grinned. "I'm still a frog."

She caught her breath as relief flooded through her. He was laughing. He hadn't been carried away by powerful emotions. He'd been play-acting the part of a fairy-tale hero. No wonder he'd halted that devastating kiss so easily. If she joined in the laughter, Billy would never know that his kiss had shaken her to the core of her being.

Catherine forced a laugh. "You've mixed up your fairy tales, Froggy. Prince Charming was the guy with the shoe fetish."

❧

Billy slid the last shingle into place with a tap of his hammer. He straightened cautiously on the barn's steep roof, then arched his head and shoulders back to work the kinks out of his spine. On every side, new shingles erupted helter-skelter from the weathered ones. The roof looked like it had a bad case of chicken pox. He stretched his back once more and sat down with his arms crossed on top of his upraised knees. From his rooftop perch, he watched Catherine without disturbing her, and without letting her know that he was watching.

During the afternoon, she had ridden the horses one at a time into the fenced arena farther up the driveway. Jumps that looked like picket fences and stonewalls and tall green hedges were scattered across the deep sand spread on the ground. When Catherine spurred the first horse toward a jump that seemed several feet too high, Billy had stopped work to watch. He held his breath, until the horse soared over the jump and touched down safely on the far side.

He'd been silly to worry. Catherine on horseback defined skill and elegance. He watched her complete the entire course of jumps before he turned back to the waiting stack of shingles.

Now, at the end of the afternoon, Catherine faced her newest pupil, the horse she called Lucky, because he didn't die in an accident on a treacherous mountain highway. Even a day later, Billy cringed as he imagined Catherine's trailer tipped on its side, the horse trapped inside, badly hurt and screaming. It had been a close call, closer than he admitted to himself at first.

He vowed to be extra careful when driving in the rain for the rest of his life, and breathed a sigh of relief as Catherine swung lightly into Lucky's saddle.

She urged the horse to step over a series of widely spaced parallel poles resting on the ground. Lucky resisted. He threw his head back dangerously close to Catherine's face and tried to jerk the reins out of her hands. He leaped sideways, trying to throw her out of the saddle. She brought the stubborn creature around to face the four-inch-high obstacle course again and again. Finally, Lucky stepped over the first pole. After he walked across the poles several times, Catherine steered him over them at an easy trot. She pulled him to a stop, patted him on the neck, and praised him.

The satisfied tone of her voice didn't match her words. "I'm so very impressed, Lucky. Just think, you might have tripped and fallen on your nose. But you stepped right over all those nasty poles. What a brave boy you are!"

A hoot of laughter came from the barn's roof. Catherine grinned up at Billy. "What's going on?"

"Just enjoying the horse show." He rose and made his way toward a ladder that leaned against the edge of the roof.

"For a while there it felt more like a war than a horse show."

Catherine watched as Billy climbed down the ladder. She studied how he stepped from one rung to the next and admired the way his faded denim jeans clung to his body. A woman would have to be dead not to notice a thing like that, she thought.

Looking at the scenery did not violate her resolve to stay at least five feet away from him at all times. After melting in his arms earlier that morning, her dignity and sanity demanded that she deal with her temporary handyman on a 'business only' basis.

"All done on the roof?" she asked. Lucky fidgeted beneath her as Billy walked across the sand toward her.

"The next storm will show whether I found all the leaks, or not, but I think that's it for now." He held out a hand toward the horse.

Before she could prevent it, Lucky spun around and aimed a kick at Billy. As he scrambled out of the way, Catherine pulled on the reins and brought the horse under control. "Watch it! Never walk up to a skittish horse."

"Sorry. I didn't realize he was nervous." Billy eyed the horse as if it had sprouted a set of horns and a forked tail.

"Why did you think he was dancing around like that?"

She leaned down and patted the horse's neck. Lucky stood quietly, as if that one show of hostility had taken the edge off his bad temper.

"I don't know much about horses," Billy admitted. "You're half Native American. You should learn."

"What about the English/Irish/French half?" He smiled up at her.

She returned Billy's smile. "Once I have the Native American half up on a horse, the motley half gets to go along for the ride."

"Okay."

"You want a riding lesson?"

"Sure. If I'm going to hang around here for a few days, I guess I should learn enough to keep from getting killed."

"More like several broken ribs. Of course, you could get killed, if a horse kicked you in the head."

"Oh, thanks, that's just great! I thought I was exaggerating." He backed away to what seemed a safer distance.

"I promise, you won't die today."

"What about broken ribs?" He had stopped fooling around.

She shook her head. "Not part of the lesson plan. Just some basics about handling horses and a ride around the arena on my most placid mare."

He looked at her, his face a picture of uncertainty. She grinned down at him. "It will be easy, you'll see."

"All right. I'll give it a try.

"Great. Let me put this horse in his stall, and then we can start your lesson."

With Catherine on her way to the barn, Billy began to chuckle, then to laugh out loud. He'd been controlling the urge ever since Catherine condemned him for neglecting his heritage.

Most people got their ideas about Native Americans from movies. Catherine was no exception. She seemed to have drawn her impression of him from recent films. In his experience, the older the movie, the uglier and more villainous were the savages. Modern westerns depicted bands of handsome, noble, half-naked, leather-clad warriors decked out in eagle feathers and face paint, galloping their horses across panoramic, photogenic, sweeping vistas of the Great Plains. Neither of those Hollywood images came close to the truth.

Billy's mother was Cherokee. Long ago, her people lived in the southern Appalachian Mountains. Not a plain in sight, Great, or otherwise. His ancestors traveled by foot and in canoes hollowed out of logs.

He wondered what Catherine would do if he carved a canoe out of one of her pine trees and offered to give her a ride around the lake. He wondered if she could swim. Just in case.

Twenty minutes later, Billy found himself sitting bareback on a red-colored horse that seemed a lot taller from on top than it had from the ground. Catherine clamped one hand on his calf just below his knee and wrapped her other hand around his ankle. She tugged his leg down with both hands, turning his foot so his toes pointed away from the horse's ribs.

"Push down into your heels and grip the horse with your calves," she ordered.

Billy sucked in a shallow breath between clenched teeth. The horse had a knife for a backbone. He shifted to one side and lost his balance. If Catherine hadn't grabbed his leg again he would have been down on the ground eating dirt. "Ah," Billy began, "some stuff I'm fond of is getting mashed."

"Men have been riding horses for centuries," Catherine informed him.

"They had saddles."

"You can't use stirrups while you're wearing running shoes." When she saw that he was about to argue with her, she said, "Well, you could, but it would be really dangerous. If you fall, your foot could get caught in the stirrup. Believe me, being dragged by a panic-stricken horse is not something you want to experience."

"Believe me, castration isn't either!"

"Don't be ridiculous. Just pull your shoulders back and sit up straight!"

He did as she instructed and struggled to keep his balance as the horse jogged slowly in a circle around Catherine. The picture that Catherine had painted of a panic-stricken horse was fresh in his mind. He knew the only things that kept the horse from jumping over the arena fence and racing breakneck across the meadow toward the lake was a long rope hitched it its bridle and the questionable strength of a willowy, blond girl. Billy did not feel particularly safe.

He clutched the reins in sweaty hands and concentrated on keeping Catherine happy. She had scolded him already for jerking on the reins, for letting his heels rise higher than his toes, for slouching, and for not looking where he was going. The list of his faults was long. He'd never felt so uncoordinated in his life.

After half an hour, Catherine called a halt to the lesson. "Time to stop."

"Hey," Billy objected, "I was just getting the hang of it."

She shook her head. "You're going to feel it tomorrow, as it is. If you end up too saddle sore to walk, I doubt you'll ever climb on a horse again."

Billy wondered how he could be saddle sore if Catherine hadn't let him use a saddle, but she was the boss. He swung his leg over the horse's rump and let himself slide to the ground.

When his feet touched the soft sand of the arena, his knees wobbled. Unknown muscles announced their presence by sending little zinging twinges up and down his thighs.

Catherine unclipped her lead rope from the mare's bridle and pulled the reins over the horse's head. The horse stood motionless. Billy thought she must feel relieved to have him off her back, after all the bouncing he'd done.

"Here." Catherine handed the knotted ends of the reins to him. "Walk her around the arena to cool her down. Then I'll groom her and put her in her stall."

She strolled off, leaving him with more than a thousand pounds of horse connected to the thin strips of leather he held in his hand. He had no idea what to do next. He took a tentative step and, to his relief, the horse moved forward with him.

As he led the horse through the deepening evening shadows, Billy decided he liked the slow pace of life on the farm. There were moments of solitude like this one in which he could mull things over without interference from fellow musicians bent on settling artistic differences with their fists. Come to think of it, Billy recalled with a smile, John knew even more bad words than Carl did. Sometime soon, a few days from now, he would return to the mansion and have a nice loud shouting match with the hot-tempered guitar player. Then he and John would get back to work on their music. He'd miss the farm even more once he was back in the hectic world of the music business. Billy shrugged and walked faster. The horse followed willingly.

Banishing any more thoughts of business from his mind, he considered Catherine. Around her horses she became confident and capable, and very different from the novice he'd kissed that morning in the barn. He pictured her eyes, dark with desire, gazing into his while he bent to capture her lips. He remembered the touch of her hands at the back of his neck as she freed his hair and gave herself just as freely to an unemployed almost car thief named William Caldwell, not to the world-famous musician named Billy Raven. And that summed up his situation. The car thief wanted to make love to Catherine, while the musician's sense of honor stopped him. The whole thing would have been laughable, if there hadn't been something about Catherine that fascinated him and kept him from returning to his career. Billy sighed. He saw Catherine making her way back to the arena and knew all too well what it meant to be trapped in a lie.

Catherine took the mare from Billy's keeping. She watched him walk away with a sense of loss. Soon he'd be gone from her life without a backward glance.

He'd been friendly, but completely impersonal following their encounter in the barn. That proved he wasn't attracted to her. And thank goodness for that! she thought. His lack of interest had saved her from making an absolute fool of herself over a single kiss.

In the shadows of the barn, Catherine moved a brush over the mare's dusty coat while her thoughts drifted to the past. As her mother's personal assistant, always dressed in fashion forward designer suits and shoes, she had gotten plenty of male attention. But the fame of her parents made their flattery suspect. Pretty speeches and sincerity were miles apart, more often than not. She couldn't remember the last time she'd accepted an invitation to dinner, or to a movie, or to a concert. A long time, anyway.

More reserved than the rest of her family, she didn't think of herself as an introvert. She could hold her own in conversations with members of the international elite, as well as with the gum-chewing cashier at the local hardware store. Most people found her company agreeable. But not Billy. He'd teased her, criticized her, and disrupted her routine. He'd kissed her. Then he'd stepped back as if nothing had happened, leaving her obsessed with him and floundering in a swamp of troubling questions. Why have I never fallen in love? Why have I never been swept off my feet by romance? When did I become so suspicious of men?

The answers seemed simple. Burdened by her parents' needs, she had ignored her own needs. But more than that, none of the men she met in the past seemed the least bit attractive. All of them fluttered around her mother and father like moths drawn by their brilliance.

At the time, she had focused on her mother's lack of affection and respect for her. Now, a moment's thought convinced Catherine that loneliness had played a large part in her decision to begin a new life away from her parents.

So, what had she done? Entirely free to make her own choices for the first time, she had thrown herself at the most unsuitable man she could find. And he had rejected her! If she wanted someone to love, why had she picked someone who was impossible? But she had picked Billy, and within hours she had fallen in love with him, insane as that might seem to her.

Soon she would be alone with him in her apartment, sitting across from him at her kitchen table, pretending indifference she didn't feel. She wasn't sure she could pull off such a difficult deception.

Four

Catherine stopped in the open door of her apartment to take in the scene. Billy was lounging on her bed. He had kicked off his dusty running shoes, leaving his long, narrow feet in not-quite-white crew socks. His legs were crossed at his ankles. He leaned against a stack of her pillows with his hands behind his head. He was the picture of relaxation. The picture would have made an excellent advertisement for a mattress company. A sitcom filled the nearby television screen. Catherine noticed that it was a repeat of one of her favorite shows.

When she stepped through the doorway into the room, Billy waggled one crew-socked foot in greeting and smiled at her. The smile on his face looked a little too assured, a little too self-satisfied. Catherine's doubts about spending the evening with him fell away. With a smile of her own, she decided to protect herself from Billy by wiping that smug smile off his face.

In a neutral tone of voice, she said, "It seems I haven't given you enough work to do to keep you busy."

Billy's pleased expression began to fade. He straightened to a sitting position and dropped his feet to the floor. "What do you mean?"

She folded her arms over her chest and looked at him from under her brows. "You're in here without my permission."

He frowned, his self-assurance gone. "I didn't think you would mind."

"For all I know," she purred, "you've invaded more than my bedroom."

"What's that supposed to mean?" He was beginning to sound uneasy and defensive.

"You've had plenty of time to snoop through all my things, while I was out in the barn."

"Now wait one minute!" He catapulted off the bed, his face growing red, his eyes narrowed to slits.

Catherine burst out in peals of laughter at his outraged expression.

He shook his head, grinned at her, and said, "Woman, you don't know how close you just came to learning a lesson that has nothing to do with sitting on a horse."

"Oh, maybe I do," she said, smiling sweetly.

He rolled his eyes at her and she laughed again. "Not nice, boss," he said, and flopped back onto her bed.

Catherine bent, pulled off her boots, and set them beside the back door before crossing over to him. She gave his feet a little shove, and he moved his legs to the side. She sat facing him at the end of the bed and leaned back against the brass foot rail. He pulled one of the pillows from the stack behind him and handed it to her. "You really don't mind me being in here without your permission?"

She lifted one shoulder in an unconcerned shrug. "I don't think I'd like it if you followed me around like a lost puppy all the time. Anyway, until you learn which end of a horse eats hay and which end kicks, you're safer right where you are." Her grin was wicked.

"You don't believe in letting a guy off easy, do you?" He raised both hands palms up in surrender. "I confess. I'm completely incompetent when it comes to any animal with more than two feet, especially an animal that outweighs me by hundreds of pounds."

"Oh, so true!" She chuckled. "I will never forget watching you try to mount a horse for the first time. Actually, the second time. The first time you went all the way over the mare's back and off the other side."

"Don't remind me." He still had grit in his hair from the incident. He covered his eyes with one hand and groaned, then shifted awkwardly on the bed, trying to find a more comfortable position.

Catherine frowned and said, "I was afraid of that."

"What?"

"That you would be saddle sore. I probably should have ended your lesson sooner."

"I'll live," Billy grumbled.

"Good," she said, with a nod.

It was Catherine sitting inches from him on the bed, not the ache in his butt, that pained him. She had surprised him when she joined him. Not that he minded sharing the bed with her. He liked the idea, maybe too much. Catherine, relaxed and teasing, tempted him. A trail of pale freckles, little sun-kissed dapples, disappeared under the material of her open shirt collar. He wondered where they might lead him, if he traced them with his tongue. He nearly groaned out loud again.

His struggle to keep his hands off of her became infinitely more difficult when she was this close to him.

Then, as if reading his mind, she scurried off the bed toward the kitchen side of the room. "Maybe it would help, if I fed you. How about soup and sandwiches?" She pulled a saucepan from the cupboard and set it on the stovetop.

"Sounds fine." He was hungry enough to eat the horse that was responsible for his aching backside.

"Minestrone, or chicken noodle?" She brandished a can opener at him.

"I'm injured and bedridden. It has to be chicken noodle," he said.

"Poor fragile man," Catherine jeered cheerfully.

Billy gave her a wan smile. "I believe I could swallow a sip or two, if you bring it to me here on my death bed." He wiggled his eyebrows at her.

Catherine burst out laughing. She'd never met anyone who made her laugh so easily, at least not anyone who didn't have a career on the stage. "You really should be an actor instead of a carpenter."

"Thanks, but no thanks. Not my gig." Billy shrugged. He wasn't counting the seven music videos he'd filmed.

He enjoyed acting, but not enough to pursue it as a separate career. Music consumed him heart and soul. Making movies seemed bland by comparison. Still, he felt pleased that he had entertained Catherine.

"I suppose you get a lot of satisfaction out of working with your hands." She poured the can of chicken soup into a saucepan and turned up the heat.

"I like to build things."

She smiled at him. "How about building some sandwiches while I improve the soup." He found the ingredients for peanut butter and jelly sandwiches and spread them out on the kitchen counter. He was a master at PBJs. He'd been making them since he was four, or five years old.

While he plastered goo on thick slices of whole wheat bread, his attention was on Catherine, and how much he enjoyed doing simple tasks with her standing at his side.

Billy watched as she took a bottle from the cupboard overhead and added a splash of sherry to the soup. She bent to check the height of the gas flame, and adjusted it lower so it barely flickered. She gave the soup a gentle stir.

When she noticed Billy watching her, she explained, "I'm warming the sherry without boiling away all the pizzazz."

"Good trick," he said, wondering if he would ever again eat bargain brand canned soup. He went back to work on the sandwiches, gluing the slices of bread together in leaky pairs, with raspberry jam oozing out the sides, and stacking them on a couple of plates.

Catherine poured the soup into mugs and handed one to Billy.

He studied the hard wooden chairs flanking the dining table. "Do you mind if I take my food over to the bed?" he asked. "I wasn't kidding about having a sore butt."

"Sure, I guess..."

Billy took his mug and plate of sandwiches and made a beeline for the bed, leaving Catherine standing by the table holding her spoon.

"Come on. There's a good show on TV," he invited.

Catherine hesitated. She had managed to hide her distressing attraction to Billy by teasing him, and he reacted by making her laugh. Yet, jokes and good-natured needling only went so far as a buffer between her fantasies and the very real man relaxing on her bed. She knew she had to join him, or look ridiculous, sitting alone at the table. She sighed, squared her shoulders, and marched resolutely across the room.

Catherine sat as far away from Billy as she could manage on a full size mattress. She folded her legs to one side and leaned again against the brass rail at the foot of the bed. After a few minutes, even with the pillow she used before, the metal rail dug into her back. She leaned against it anyway so she couldn't possibly touch Billy by accident. She was afraid that touching him would demolish the last shreds of her self-control. She tried not to imagine what she might do if that happened here in her cramped apartment, on her comfortable bed. She felt the metal rail pressing against her spine and was glad to feel something besides desire. The pain was a small price to pay for hanging onto her dignity. And her sanity.

Billy's attention seemed to be focused on the television show. She took a sip of her soup and then a bite of her sandwich. Her anxiety began to ease. Moments later, she glanced over at him and discovered she'd been wrong. He was watching her.

"What?" she asked, not really sure of what she was asking.

After a short pause, he said, "Chicken pizzazz soup is pretty good." He smiled at her, but she had the feeling that he had been thinking about something else.

During the next commercial break, she carried their empty dishes to the sink, where she ran some warm water over them and left them to soak. Before she could dry her hands and return to her place at the end of the bed, Billy sprang to his feet and strolled toward her.

"I have something in mind," he said.

Awareness shimmied its way up Catherine's spine. Her eyes followed him as he prowled closer. When he eased around the dining table, her breath seeped away. She stared at him, not asking what he meant, or what he intended.

"Something tempting..." His voice was as smooth as the velvety coat of a newborn foal. She stood riveted, gazing at him. No power imaginable, not even one of San Francisco's legendary earthquakes, could have moved her from the spot. The barn could have fallen to the ground around her and she wouldn't have been able to save herself.

He stepped even closer. "...and unexpected."

He reached out and drew a tumbled lock of her hair through his fingers, then tucked it behind her ear. When his hand fell away, she managed to gather her wits just enough to ask, "What are you talking about?"

"Caramel corn. I noticed a huge can of the stuff up in the cupboard, where you keep the sherry." He cocked a dark brow at her. "What did you think I was talking about?"

"Nothing, absolutely nothing at all!" He'd been thinking about dessert, while all she could think about was kissing him. She felt her cheeks growing warm, and began to study the way her thick wool socks made her ankles look fat.

"So, how about it?" he asked. "Do we open the popcorn and pig out while we catch a movie? Or do I make my way through the freezing night to my very narrow and too short bed?" She looked up at him, and he grinned at her.

Catherine sighed. Unforeseen problems kept falling in front of her like an endless row of tilting dominoes. When she offered Billy the temporary job of live-in handyman, she hadn't given a bit of thought to how he would spend his evenings. The deserted house was as bleak and uninviting as a house could be. She couldn't expect him to sit in her brother's studio for hours on end with nothing to do but watch the candles burn low. She was forced to admit that sexual attraction was a very poor substitute for forethought and planning.

Worse, her infatuation with him had nothing to do with the way Billy behaved toward her. He hadn't done anything to encourage her, except be friendly and helpful. He could fall off a horse and sprawl flat on his face in the dirt, and still she desired him. Her fantasies about Billy were making her tense and unhappy, and keeping her from enjoying the things he did offer to her.

Things like lively conversation and his sense of humor. Her runaway feelings were a problem that she needed to confront and put an end to once and for all.

She forced a laugh. "It has to be the popcorn," she said.

"Great. Have you got any napkins?"

Catherine tore a handful of paper towels from the roll sitting on the kitchen counter and plodded after Billy.

He picked up the remote and began flipping through cable channels faster than her eyes could focus, leaving her slightly dizzy. She dropped the paper towels in a heap in the middle of the mattress and took up her former position at the end of the bed. She stared at the heap of towels and imagined that it was a fence topped by barbed wire. With attack dogs patrolling the area inside.

She was determined to stay on her side of the fence. She pulled her knees close to her chest and wrapped her arms around her bent legs. There was space now between her and the pile of paper towels. Sitting tied in knots was uncomfortable, but necessary if she wanted to have a chance to survive the next couple of hours without embarrassing herself beyond any redemption.

"What'll it be?" he asked, glancing up at her. "We have a choice of action, romance, or subtitles on the foreign film channel."

Instantly, she said, "Action." A romantic movie in her unbalanced state of mind could be her ruin. And you never knew, with foreign films, when you might end up with scenes that had more nudity than dialogue. Watching Billy watch an action movie was temptation enough.

"How about the original Terminator? It just started."

"Okay." As a teenager, she and Sin had gone to a revival of the movie in a theater in San Francisco. They had stuffed themselves with buttered popcorn. Apparently, the movie and popcorn went together.

She remembered that Arnold Schwarzenegger had slashed his way across Los Angeles, mowing down innocent victims right and left. If she closed her eyes to shut out temptation, Billy was sure to think that extreme violence was her only reason.
Curled in her cramped position, it wasn't long before her foot went to sleep. Darting pains ran from her ankle down to her toes. Fences and attack dogs vanished from her mind.

She unwound her arms from around her bent knees and straightened her legs. The sudden increase in circulation brought an even sharper pain. She leaned forward and began to rub her foot.

After a moment, Billy's hands drew hers away. He lifted her foot onto his thigh and used just the right amount of pressure to bring relief, and turn her pain into something dangerously sensual.

Catherine recognized an expert's touch. With his amazing good looks, knowing how to massage women's feet probably went with the territory. The sensation of Billy's hands on her sped her heart and made her catch her breath. She tried to tug her foot out of his grasp. "Let go!"

His fingers tightened. "Pardon me?"

She looked down at the quilt that covered the bed and mumbled, "I mean...uh...thanks. It feels okay now."

He released her, letting his fingers slide across the sole of her foot. Her head snapped up, and she stared at him. A slight smile played at his lips. "You're welcome. Enjoying the film?"

"Yes, very much." The bland conversation did nothing to ease her anxiety. In fact, it was making it worse. Why is he smiling at me that way? She wished he'd go back to watching the movie.

She turned toward the television screen and tried to sound enthusiastic, "Oh, this is one of my favorite parts!"

Then she actually looked at the scene playing out on the screen, and frowned. An angry police officer was badgering the handcuffed hero. To tell the truth, Catherine didn't recognize the scene. She should have been paying more attention to the story before she blurted out the first stupid thing that came into her head.

"Mine too," Billy said.

⁓

Puzzled, Catherine glanced at him. He seemed caught up in the film once again. In the lobby of the police station, Schwarzenegger leaned toward the clueless desk sergeant and promised, "I'll be back."

The line had become part of American culture. Catherine remembered that the lull in the action was about to end as a car crashed through the police station's front doors. She leaned back against her pillow and watched Billy as he watched the film. He paid no attention to her. She decided that she should stop making a fool of herself and stretched out on the bed. It wasn't long before her eyes closed and she drifted off to sleep.

Billy munched a handful of popcorn and watched Catherine sleep. The little worry lines that grooved her forehead during the day had vanished. Her hair lay like a tangle of sunshine around her face. This morning she compared herself to Cinderella, she was Sleeping Beauty tonight. If she knew his real name, he could awaken her with a kiss.

A ripple of pure desire flowed through him. He rode with it this time, not needing to hide it from Catherine. His feelings for her had changed. They had grown both more complex and, at the same time, more direct and simple.

He wanted her. In a few days he would explain all his evasions and half-truths. She would be embarrassed that she hadn't recognized him, and very angry. Furious. He knew he was in for the tongue lashing of his life. After that, after Catherine calmed down, he'd court her. Maybe he'd take her to Texas to meet his family. But until she knew the truth, he would be patient. Very, very patient.

He watched the end of the movie.

A silver Mercedes coupe, glinting in the morning sunlight, passed through the rusty gate and purred up the curving drive. From his seat on the wooden swing deep within the old house's shadowed porch, Billy watched the car roll to a stop near the open barn door. The driver stepped out of the car and stood staring down at her shoes. Then she tiptoed across the muddy ground toward the door, not once letting her high heels touch the earth. Watching her, Billy imagined a ballerina crossing a stage covered with writhing cobras. Grinning, he sipped his second cup of Catherine's freshly brewed coffee, and made a guess as to the identity of the visitor.

Breakfast with Catherine had been interesting. She apologized several times for falling asleep during the movie and leaving him to his own devices. She avoided mentioning the fact that he had stripped off her jeans and tucked her into bed, without waking her. While he ate thick slices of French toast dripping with butter and sweet clover honey, she toyed with her food and kept glancing toward the bed.

Evidence of last night's activity was nowhere to be seen. All of the pillows were back at the head of the bed and the quilt lay as smooth as the surface of an ice rink. Catherine's glances were anything but cool. Her cheeks glowed pink with every furtive glance.

Repeated apologies aside, Billy knew she was more embarrassed by him seeing her lace-trimmed panties than by any failures she may have had as a hostess. He thought the lace-trimmed panties were well worth seeing and he wasn't a bit embarrassed by having seen them. They were pale pink, a softer shade than the color of Catherine's cheeks at the moment. Deliberately teasing, he too turned to stare at the bed.

Catherine made a small choking sound, but said nothing as she slapped a second helping of French toast onto his plate. When he only smirked at her in response, she picked up a knife and began slashing the toast on her own plate into pieces the size of confetti. He'd been delighted with her reaction.

She certainly wasn't indifferent to him. Not at all. Billy gave the swing a push and took another swig of his coffee, settling back to keep an eye on developments in the barn.

Catherine fretted while she spread new straw in the stall she had just cleaned. She cringed every time she thought about Billy putting her to bed like a little child. She groaned at the thought of his dark eyes sliding over her bare legs, then lingering on the tiny strip of pink lace that covered her most intimate parts. Why couldn't I have been wearing thick, white cotton, granny panties? she lamented. She could feel his eyes on her still, as if his gaze had left an indelible impression beneath her jeans.

She shook her head at her own cowardly behavior at breakfast. After stuffing a couple of bites of French toast in her mouth, she had fled into the barn, leaving Billy to finish his breakfast by himself. She had spent the next hour shoveling dirty straw into the wheelbarrow faster than ever before. The bandana covering her hair was soaked with sweat by the time she took a break and returned to her apartment for a glass of cold water.

There, she discovered that the dishes had been washed and were drying in the rack on the counter. The coffee pot was nearly empty and a mug was missing from the rack, telling her that Billy was around somewhere having a second cup of coffee.

"Just so he stays away from me," she said to the empty room.

Then she realized that he hadn't followed her into the barn, or offered to help clean stalls. Some handyman, she thought. She ought to be angry that he was missing. Instead, she felt relieved that she didn't have to face him. She wanted to avoid a replay of yesterday's romantic encounter in the barn.

Especially now that Billy had undressed her. And looked at her. And, and...

She didn't want to imagine a single thing more.

Catherine swallowed the last of the water and dumped the ice cubes in the sink. She left her glass on the counter. Billy could wash it along with the mug he was using.

Out of habit, she checked her appearance in the mirror beside the door. Her hair hung in sweaty tangles across her face. She looked a mess and couldn't care less. Now, let Billy get an eyeful of me covered in dust and clinging bits of straw, and fully clothed. She imagined that the expression on his face then would seem nothing like desire.

When she stepped into the barn, she was no longer alone.

"So this is where you've hidden yourself," her mother said. She pushed past Catherine and stood in the doorway, inspecting the tiny apartment. "You actually live in this place?"

Catherine wondered what word her mother might have used instead of place. Slum, or dump, or trash heap seemed possible. There were other choices, all of them insulting. "Good morning, Mother," she said to the woman's back.

Her mother turned. Catherine watched as her mother's eyes slid toward the mirror that hung from a nail beside the door. As if the sight of her own face was pleasing, she now wore a slight smile. But in a tone that conveyed distaste, her mother said, "Won't you invite me in?"

"Of course," Catherine replied. "Welcome to my home."

She followed her mother to the kitchen table, expecting her to sit down. Her mother ignored the chair Catherine offered and prowled the room instead.

Finally, she faced Catherine. "So Spartan. So lacking in fashion, in comfort itself."

Catherine nearly laughed, before she brought herself under control. Her mother's behavior was outrageous. It always had been. Catherine had gained enough detachment in the past few months to see her mother for what she was, a selfish woman used to getting her own way, used to demanding what she wanted, instead of asking for it.

Catherine gazed at her mother impassively. "Why are you here, Mother?"

"Rita quit yesterday. I'm absolutely furious with her."

"Rita makes four in a row, Mother." Catherine shook her head. Her mother went through personal assistants the same way normal people used toothpaste.

"None of them can compare to you, my darling," her mother cooed. "Won't you reconsider and come back to me?"

Catherine ticked off flattery on the mental list she kept of her mother's manipulative tactics. "We've had this conversation before. I have my own business, now."

"A bunch of smelly horses and a dilapidated barn."

"From your point of view. Not from mine. I've invested all that I have to make this business a success."

"If it's a question of money, I'll double your old salary."

Catherine's mental list included bribery. "Money has nothing to do with my decision. Didn't you ever have hopes and dreams, Mother?"

"Dreams accomplish nothing. Hope is a waste of time."

When Catherine remained silent, her mother went on, adding details to her line of reasoning. "From the very beginning, I knew my first novel would be a bestseller."

No one could accuse her mother of being modest. Catherine merely shrugged and replied, "I know how to train horses."

"Without Rita to help me, I don't know which way to turn."

Her mother's voice quivered with uncertainty. That particular tactic had worked so well for so long, Catherine struggled against her first impulse, which was to leap to the rescue. Her mother's personality was a complicated combination of self-absorption, helplessness, and single-minded determination to let nothing interfere with her career as a writer. Catherine had wasted years catering to her. Finally, the daily lack of affection, the lack of simple courtesy, convinced Catherine that her mother held everyone, including her own daughter, in barely concealed contempt. Nine months had passed since Catherine handed her mother a formal letter of resignation. Nine peaceful months out of twenty-three years. Catherine's shoulders straightened, the line of her jaw firmed.

"I'm sorry you feel unhappy," she said. "I'm sorry, too, that I need to get back to work. Perhaps, if you had told me you were coming, I could have arranged for us to have a longer visit." She turned toward the door leading to the barn.

"Don't you dare walk away from me!" her mother said. "I came to talk some sense into you."

Catherine paused. "If you want to talk with me, you'll have to do it while I work."

As Billy downed the last sip of his coffee, he wondered idly what could have prompted a visit by a famous author wearing stiletto heels. He decided to make the woman's acquaintance. He set his empty mug on the wooden arm of the porch swing and ambled toward the barn.

The famous author's angry voice carried from the open door. Billy didn't like the acid tone of her voice very much, and he liked the attitude that it revealed even less. He stepped into the dusky interior of the barn, pausing to take in the situation.

A few yards down the central corridor, mother and daughter faced each other. The author's back was turned toward him. Catherine noticed him standing in the doorway and sent him a long look, acknowledging his arrival. Her dusty jeans and scuffed boots suited her surroundings. Her mother's impeccable hairstyle and trendy magenta tweed suit seemed ludicrous beside a wheelbarrow piled high with filthy straw.

Billy studied Catherine. Her face seemed a bit pale in contrast to the red bandana tied around her hair. He noted that her arms were crossed over her chest, in self-defense, or holding back anger, he couldn't tell which, while her mother shouted at her.

Catherine watched him as he came closer. The expression on her face made him want to kick something, like Mrs. O'Shea's expensively tailored magenta tweed butt. In mid-rant, she was oblivious to everything else, which allowed him to move up behind her, before he announced his presence. Billy held Catherine's gaze and was rewarded with a small smile.

"Hello," he said, making Catherine's mother jump. Score one for our side, he thought, as she whirled toward him, tipping slightly on her extravagant heels. He saw now that her shoes were fashioned from snake skin. He grinned, remembering that he had first pictured her as a ballerina surrounded by cobras. Now, he refined that image. She wasn't the ballerina, she was the cobra. He crowded closer.

The cobra held her ground and looked Billy up and down, lingering over his roughhewn features and scowling at his worn jeans and disreputable running shoes. From behind her mother's back, Catherine rolled her eyes at him.

"Now, I see why you have no time to spare for me," her mother said. She took a step to the side so she could keep both her daughter and the intruder in sight.

Catherine forced a polite response. "Mother, this is my handyman, William Caldwell." Both remained silent during the long pause that followed. Catherine knew her mother's thoughts were racing, as she searched for the correct attitude to assume.

"I'm so glad," she exclaimed to Catherine at last, "that you have hired someone to help you. That will make it so much easier for you to come work for me."

Her mother wore a pleased expression for the first time that morning. As if wishing made a thing true, Catherine thought. Her mother could wish all she wanted, Catherine had no intention of ever working for her again. "I'm afraid not," she said.

"Why, whatever do you mean?" Her mother's confusion seemed genuine for a moment, then she rallied. "Are you so selfish that you would begrudge me a few hours of your precious time each day? How am I to manage?" Her mother's hands flopped helplessly to illustrate her inability to cope.

Catherine watched Billy's jaw drop in surprised disbelief. She aimed an ironic look at him and shrugged her shoulders the slightest bit.

"Since that is the case," Catherine said, "the sooner you hire a new assistant, the better. I'd be happy to write the help wanted ad." Her offer was genuine.

"Don't bother," her mother replied, without a trace of her former helplessness. "I have the ad you wrote last year on file in my office. There is no need for you to be concerned with my affairs." She left unspoken: Not when you are so very busy with your own affair.

She cast a disdainful glance at Billy. Her look said he was obviously a nobody. Catherine knew that, to her mother's way of thinking, if Catherine had chosen him as her lover, both of them were beneath contempt.

Making the point, her mother strode straight at Billy. He dodged to one side as she marched out of the barn, leaving puncture wounds every place her heels drilled into the ground.

Catherine breathed a sigh of relief.

Billy said, "Well, Boss, what's on the 'to do' list for today?"

Five

Hidden Lake nestled in a hollow among the pines like a shiny dime cupped in a half-opened hand. The afternoon breeze brushed Catherine's cheeks in a cool kiss and gently stirred the surface of the lake. Sunlight burnished the water, turning the ripples silver against deep blue. Wavelets drifted out of the shallows to swirl against the shore and rolled lazily around her mount's hooves.

Since moving to the farm, she had paused in the same spot many times, and wished she had someone to share her pleasure. Someone who knew without being told that this place was special and should be experienced with an open heart. She had gazed at the sunlight sparkling on the water and imagined the man she would love, a man who would love her in return. She hadn't met that man, yet, and didn't know if, or when, she ever would. Today, her fantasy lover had been replaced by a friend.

She had been surprised by Billy's support during her mother's unannounced visit, and by his respect for her privacy afterward. He asked no questions about her mother. He just picked up a shovel and began cleaning a stall, drawing her back into her daily routine. They worked side-by-side in silence. As the minutes ticked past, she slowly calmed. Finally, taking a deep breath, she put the whole ugly incident behind her. She and Billy worked on through most of the morning in quiet companionship.

In the early afternoon, they rode to the lake. Billy was mounted for the second time on the red mare. Catherine rode the black stallion, Admiral, and led the way along a narrow trail through the pine forest to the lake. They paused on the lake shore to admire the view, lingering there for a while. Now, with Billy at her side, Catherine savored a moment of silent enjoyment that seemed almost perfect.

Billy thought the area around Hidden Lake was some of the loveliest country he had ever seen. Screened on one side by pine forest, on the other side the lake lapped against a low granite cliff where large blocks of stone had tumbled into the water.

A small grove of manzanitas grew near the base of the cliff, their orange trunks a vivid contrast to the darker granite. Blue jays darted among the manzanita branches. Their scolding calls were repeated with added flourishes by a mockingbird perched somewhere behind Billy in the pines. Overhead, clouds drifted across the blue sky.

"This is nice." Billy realized his words were inadequate, and he regretted them the moment he said them. His regret doubled as Catherine sighed and pointed to the trail that led through the trees to their right. "Farther around the lake, there's a spot where we can eat lunch."

She pulled her huge, black horse around and trotted off in that direction, calling over her shoulder, "Don't follow too close. Sometimes that mare still thinks she's a race horse. She might try to beat Admiral to the finish line."

Billy had learned that riding was a whole lot easier with a saddle. That morning, after cleaning the barn and feeding the horses, Catherine had taken him shopping. The change of scene had done them both good. Catherine seemed happier and back to being the person he'd first met, an independent woman who was hard-working and upbeat.

While Catherine bought new window panes for the barn at the hardware store, Billy roamed the aisles of the thrift shop across the street. He figured his ragged appearance and the location itself would protect his identity. Billy Raven, rock star, did not wear used clothing.

He'd found a flannel shirt, jeans, socks, and briefs by the time Catherine joined him. He had enough cash to cover the bill, with a bit to spare, and remembered how much he enjoyed finding a bargain, before he became a famous millionaire. He grinned at Catherine. "All this stuff was less than eighteen bucks."

When Catherine offered to buy him boots, Billy argued against it, saying he wouldn't need them once his work on the farm was done. Catherine called him stubborn and pointed out that he would be more help with boots on his feet than without. The boots he chose were badly worn. Catherine called them well-loved and laughed at him when he tried them on. As the red mare walked along the path beside the lake, Billy wiggled his toes in his brand new, second-hand, broken down boots, and decided that courting Catherine was going to be much more fun than he first imagined.

Billy urged the mare around the last bend in the trail and rode out of the tree shade into bright sunlight where Catherine waited. He kicked his feet free of his stirrups, jumped to the ground, and paused to gaze at the unspoiled landscape around him. "Wow, this is fantastic!"

Hidden from the opposite shore by fallen rocks, a patch of grass reached down to the lake's edge. The same group of manzanitas he'd seen before grew at the far end of the miniature meadow. Disturbed by his noisy arrival, a pair of chipmunks skittered through the fallen leaves and vanished among the crowded trunks.

He turned and placed the mare's reins in Catherine's outstretched hand. She tethered their horses to a tree and then pulled a rolled blanket from behind her saddle. She tossed the blanket to him.

"Where do you want this?" he asked.

"Somewhere out of the wind. How about over there?" She pointed to a patch of thick grass growing beside a chunk of granite that sat at the edge of the lake. The weathered rock looked like an enormous troll that had been turned to stone by a passing wizard as it stooped to drink. With a little imagination, Billy could make out a face twisted in surprise. Billy sympathized.

He smiled to himself as he considered the truth of the old saying that opposites attract. In the last thirty hours, he'd been surprised more than once by the power of his attraction to Catherine. He felt even more surprised that the attraction was more than sexual.

Billy shook his head at the fix he was in. He unrolled the blanket and sat down. Catherine carried bulging leather saddle bags over to the blanket and joined him. He leaned back against the stone troll and watched Catherine unpack their lunch. She made a frustrated sound as she struggled to open a jar of pickles.

"Let me." He reached for the jar and gave the lid a sharp twist. It came off too easily. He smirked at her.

"I loosened that lid, first," she claimed, then plucked the jar out of his hand and put a sandwich in its place.

He lifted a corner of the bread and examined the filling with satisfaction. Not a repeat of last night's peanut butter and jelly. He took a bite of whole wheat and roast beef and licked some mayonnaise from his fingers. They'd stopped at the local market on the way home from the thrift store and had added a few things to Catherine's kitchen. Things that were not yogurt and canned soup. He lay down and propped himself on one elbow to smile up at her.

Catherine caught herself returning his smile a little too warmly, and shifted her gaze to the glittering water of the lake. A green and brown mallard, its iridescent feathers bright in the sunlight, paddled out from among the cattails, dragging a blue wake across the silvery ripples. She watched until the duck dived beneath the surface.

Her eyes slid back toward Billy of their own accord. He looked so darn sexy lying next to her, she found it difficult not to stare. She remembered the texture of his long hair, like warm silk sliding between her fingers. Her lips remembered the mastery of his mouth. The temptation to kiss him again became almost overpowering.

She scooted away from him, retreating until she felt the granite block at her back. She leaned against the sun-warmed stone and took a bite of pickle. The sour flavor puckered her lips. Kiss that if you dare, she challenged Billy silently with a look. The glint in his eye made her wonder if he could read her mind. He reached out and fished a pickle from the jar. When he bit into it, the face he made was exaggerated and comical. Her tension dissolved in laughter.

Finished with her lunch, Catherine let her head rest against the stone. She stared at the sky. Clouds piled one upon the other the way they often did prior to a storm, but sunlight still dominated. She had hours yet to enjoy the day. And to train horses, she reminded herself, as thoughts of her obligations intruded into these stolen moments with Billy. She promised herself that she would get back to work soon. Now, she wanted to feel the sun on her face and the breeze blowing cool and steady off the lake. She wanted more than companionship. She wanted Billy. But that was impossible.

Billy's hand closed over her leg. "Look," he whispered and pointed toward a spot a few yards away. The pair of chipmunks had invited themselves to the picnic. The tiny creatures darted ever closer to a few corn chips that had spilled across the blanket from the open bag.

Catherine froze at Billy's touch. His hand lay warm and relaxed on her leg, while his entire attention was turned toward the chipmunks. Every nerve in her body was riveted on the man beside her.

The bravest of the chipmunks stood on its hind legs, as if calculating the distance to the food and the amount of danger it faced in trying to get it. His partner crouched in the long grass, its head and the tip of its twitching, white-striped tail just visible. Two pairs of black, button eyes were fixed on the corn chips. The bold one darted onto the blanket, seized a chip in its mouth, and dashed out of reach. The second chipmunk scurried behind the first back into the trees.

"That was great!" Billy rose to his knees and peered at the place where the tiny thieves had vanished. He looked happy as a kid with a birthday bicycle.

Catherine was eaten up by desire. She clasped her hands together to keep them from reaching into forbidden territory to touch him. Her fingers ached from the effort it took.

"I think we better pack up and get going." Her voice sounded flat to her own ears.

"What's the matter?" Billy asked.

"It's time to go, that's all."

He stared at her in a way that made her want to squirm. "Don't go all silent on me. What's bothering you?"

"Nothing is bothering me, I have work to do."

"You're not a very good liar." He sat back down on the blanket.

"What are you talking about?"

"You build better walls than any brick layer I ever knew."

Catherine shook her head. "I don't have to defend myself to you, or anyone."

"No, you don't." He dragged a hand across his bearded chin and down his throat.

"I don't understand," Catherine said.

"Understand this." He reached out and hauled her onto his lap. His mouth took hers with an urgency that stunned her. He made a sound, a low tone, the sound of desire.

Catherine felt the rough wool blanket beneath her back, and the astonishing weight of Billy's body covering hers. His teeth and tongue seduced. His hands fisted in her hair, keeping her from pulling away while he nipped at her lips in such an exciting way she found herself wanting more. She welcomed the rasp of his beard against her cheeks, and met the thrust of his tongue with little forays of her own. Her hands slid over his shirt, as if gauging the width of his shoulders. She felt feminine and fragile as he held her within the leashed strength of his arms. His scent was intoxicating. She turned her head and trailed her lips down the side of his neck, tasting his skin with the tip of her tongue. Her gesture drew another hungry sound from him. When he planted his elbows on the blanket and rose over her, she no longer cared that he was unemployed and too casual with other people's property.

The angular structure of his face stood out boldly. His eyes glinted with a knowledge she both feared and desired. He could teach her, if she dared.

"Enough?" he asked.

"No," she said on a sigh.

She was far out of her league with him, Billy knew. She tempted, so sweet, so innocent, so damn virginal, she hadn't known how to kiss properly until he'd taught her just now. He wanted to teach her everything. But not today. Not until she knew his real name and accepted who and what he was.

He strung brief, wet kisses along her jaw and down the side of her neck to the point where her pulse raced. He ran his tongue over the spot and felt her shiver. Then he buried his face in the open collar of her shirt, lured there by the perfume of her skin.

"Just a little more," he promised, and planted a lingering kiss where the delicate bones met at the base of her throat.

Billy raised his head and looked at her. He'd played havoc with her hair. It framed her face in a mass of wild curls. Her eyes glowed blue as an evening sky, both shadowed and luminous. Her breath hitched in shallow gasps, as if she had run down the forest path to tumble here in his arms. He unbuttoned her shirt and drew his fingers lightly over the swell of her breasts, moving aside the lacy edge of her bra. She shifted beneath him as his lips followed the path made by his fingers. Catherine moaned and lifted her hips against him. He allowed himself permission to press his hardness into the soft juncture of her thighs, letting her feel his arousal for the first time. She didn't push him away. Her hands clung to his shirt, gathering the material against his back. Time to stop, he told himself, or they wouldn't stop, and there would be hell to pay afterward.

With difficulty, with hands that shook from an overload of sexual urgency, he pulled the edges of her shirt together and kissed her on the forehead. Then he moved to the side and cradled her in his arms. Answers to questions, and Catherine was sure to ask them, would have to wait, until he cooled down enough to string more than two words together.

Catherine thought her heart would batter its way out of her chest. She spread a limp hand across the place to slow its hectic beating. She felt lightheaded. If Billy hadn't been holding her, she thought she might float off the blanket-covered earth into the blue universe that hovered just overhead. She stared up past the gathering clouds and knew she'd never been kissed before today. Never held in someone's arms. Never touched tenderly. If this was what love felt like, then she had never loved anyone the way she loved Billy at that moment. She took a trembling breath.

He must have felt the tremor, because he stroked a hand through her hair, smoothing it off her face. "Shhh," he murmured, "everything is all right."

Catherine turned her face toward him, and he snuggled her close with her cheek resting in the hollow of his shoulder. His hand tangled in her hair. She felt his chest expand as he drew in a deep breath. He blew it out and said, "I won't apologize. I've wanted to do that since last night."

Catherine frowned. He thought I needed an apology? She realized then how naïve and inept she must seem to him. Why did he kiss me like that? What in the world does he see in me? Is this just another of his jokes? Has he been entertaining himself at my expense? All her insecurities sprang to life. She lifted her head from his shoulder and stared into his face. His eyes were closed, unreadable. "Why me?" she asked.

"Why not?" He looked at her, his expression serene. "There's something between us. You feel it, too."

"What if I do?" He hadn't offered the reassurance she hoped for. If he felt even a small part of what she felt for him, he hadn't said so.

Instead, he said, "Then stop holding back and go with it."

Catherine spoke with as much dignity as she could muster while nestled half on top of him. "I wasn't aware that I held anything back a few minutes ago."

"When I kiss you, you respond. When I'm not kissing you, a bulldozer couldn't get past all the bricks you pile up."

Catherine could hardly contain her outrage. The conversation had traveled full circle. Billy was back to accusing her of being defensive and a bad liar. She shoved against his chest. "Let me up!"

His arms tightened. "I don't think so."

She twisted in his grasp, trying to free herself. "I said, let me go!"

He rolled her onto her back and leaned over her. "Not until we talk."

His arms were steel, his voice as hard and dangerous as the granite cliff looming over them. She began to struggle.

An enraged male voice bellowed, "Get your damn hands off her!" At the same time, a foot shod in an expensive running shoe connected with Billy's shoulder and knocked him sideways. From flat on his back, Billy gazed first at the sketchpad abandoned in the grass, then up at the menacing figure of Catherine's older brother. Billy felt glad that children's book illustrators didn't carry guns.

"Sin!" Catherine bolted to her feet. She took a step in her brother's direction, then she veered toward Billy sprawled on the blanket, and choked out his name. "Billy...?"

The day had turned into an O'Shea family reunion. Billy glanced from flustered sister to furious brother and decided to stay right where he was.

Sinjin O'Shea reached out and dragged Catherine to his side. Billy noted that she seemed unsteady and blamed himself. He opened his mouth to apologize, but a blazing look from the man towering over him made him snap it shut.

O'Shea's eyes traveled over his sister's clothing. It didn't do Billy's case any good that her shirt hung limp and unbuttoned, and that her face and lips bore the marks of what looked like rough handling. O'Shea moved toward Billy.

Catherine put a restraining hand on her brother's arm. "Sin, it's not what you imagine."

Billy relaxed and smiled up at her. "Takes after his mother, doesn't he?"

When Catherine returned his smile, he pushed himself up to rest on his elbows. He wasn't going to get to his feet until the possibility of a fist fight was long past. You don't convince a woman to trust you by making hamburger out of her adored brother.

Sin stared at Billy with an odd expression on his face. "Cath, who is this guy?"

"Oh, sorry! Sin, this is William Caldwell, my handyman. He's been working on the barn."

"That's not all he's been working on, if you ask me." The comment came with a sneer.

Catherine cried, "Nothing happened!"

Billy flinched at the anxiety in her voice. Instead of calming her brother, she was making the situation worse.

"Sure." Sin sounded anything but convinced. He dropped a hand onto his sister's shoulder and turned her slightly away from Billy. "Why don't you take those horses back to the barn? I'd like to have a word with...ah...William."

When Catherine shot him a worried glance, Billy nodded and climbed to his feet. "Nothing to worry about, just talk," he assured her. "We won't even raise our voices."

Once Catherine was mounted on her horse, with the red mare in tow, Billy raised a hand in farewell. "I'll see you back at the barn in a few minutes."

"See that you do," she instructed him sternly.

As a parting shot, Billy thought it was a pretty good one. With four words she had confirmed her position as his employer, no doubt to dispel any concerns her brother might have.

Billy watched her ride off through the trees, then turned to the younger man. "Nice to see you again."

Sin stuck his fists in his pockets. "What game are you playing with my sister, Raven?"

It began raining heavily as Catherine put her spurs to the dapple gray's sides and finished the series of jumps at breakneck speed. She was soaked by the time she rode the horse out of the arena toward the barn. Catherine shivered and wished she could stand under a hot shower, but that would have to wait. The dapple gray was sweating from his workout. To cool him, she led him up and down the barn's central corridor, knowing only a fool would close a hot, sweaty horse in a cold stall. It was a perfect way to end up with a sick animal and hundreds of dollars in vet bills.

As she trudged the length of the corridor, Catherine wondered what could have happened between her brother and Billy after she left them at the lake. When they returned to the barn, they seemed to have forged a friendship. The phrase, "thick as thieves," came to mind. There was something puzzling about the way they got along with each other. Not to mention that Sin kept shooting odd glances at her. Later, when Billy sought her out, her brother tagged after him like a curious puppy. The grin on Sin's face as he listened to Billy begin an apology had been enough for her to point to the gate and order her brother out of the arena. He laughed like the idiot she'd just called him, and jogged off toward the old house.

With her brother out of the way, Billy presented her with a renewed problem. Sometime during their visit to the lake, she stopped thinking of him as a friend. Admittedly, that idea had been very recent, and contradicted both her feelings and all of their passionate kisses. Left alone together in the arena, Billy kissed her fingertips, one after the other, repeating after each nibbling caress of his lips how very sorry he was for being so rough with her. He beguiled, and aroused her. The man's mouth was wicked and he knew how to use it. Catherine had shivered then, and she shivered again now, but not due to the cold. And that was only part of her problem with Billy.

When she set aside the powerful sexual attraction she felt for him, she found that she liked him. He could be charming. His appreciation of the serene beauty of Hidden Lake couldn't have been closer to what she once imagined in a lover. His uninhibited joy at the antics of the two chipmunks had delighted her. He was hardworking and kept busy doing needed repairs around the farm. That seemed to be enough evidence to say that he tried to earn his own way, when he could. And his body? Gorgeous.

Catherine sighed. For a few minutes she let her mind drift, remembering the desire in Billy's dark eyes as his mouth lowered to hers.

Then they had argued. About her defensiveness. Catherine's footsteps slowed as she realized, quite suddenly, that she kept more things from her unhappy past than lingerie and cosmetics. She'd grown up on guard against being hurt, on guard against constant rejection that wasn't deliberate and wasn't spoken of. She stood in the middle of the corridor, holding the dapple gray's reins, certain that Billy had done nothing to make her mistrust him. It was she who owed him the apology.

She hugged the dapple gray's silky neck and rested her cheek against his warm hide. She closed her eyes for a moment, filled with quiet resolve. It wasn't too late. She would ask Billy to forgive her stupid behavior. With a little effort on her part, everything would be all right again.

Sin had made him pay, big time, for keeping his secret and for services rendered as a silent fellow conspirator. Upstairs in the ice-cold studio, Billy posed for dozens of sketches, shirtless and freezing, with one of Catherine's bandanas tied around his head. The pose and his naked chest fit Sin's idea of a pirate.

After the first hour, Billy began to wonder if an evil sneer might be etched across his face for the rest of his life. When he complained that his neck was getting stiff and his goose bumps had grown goose bumps of their own, Sin produced his own version of an evil sneer and told him to get used to it. This sitting was only the first of many, many to come. Smirking, Sin informed him that most picture books had thirty-two pages.

Billy chuckled. Sin was another single-minded O'Shea down to his toenails. And a damn fine artist. It was an honor to pose for him. But Sin would be the last to know Billy felt anything but discomfort and annoyance. It would take all the pleasure out of Sin's attempted blackmail.

Billy had complained right up to the moment Catherine's brother dashed out into the rain and loaded his sketchbooks and himself into his vintage Rolls Royce. If Sin had been delighted by his victim's performance, Billy was doubly so.

After Sin's car sped out of the gate and onto the country road, Billy headed to the barn to look for Catherine. He found her in the shower. Steam rose above the yellow curtain as she sang a classic country song, loudly and off-key. Billy winced as she tried for a high note, and failed by several tones on the musical scale. He stifled a laugh while he looked with interest at the pink robe she'd hung from a hook within easy reach of the shower. The robe was made out of the same bumpy, fuzzy material he'd seen used for bedspreads. Catherine the Practical, he acknowledged with a nod of his head. No silk or satin for the former princess. Just hard work and, afterward, a hot shower.

For a moment, he fantasized about stripping and joining her beneath the spray of warm water. He imagined her shock and protests. He imagined her melting in his arms and returning his kisses. He imagined her hands running over his wet skin. He ordered his lurid imagination to stop torturing him. Then he retreated to her apartment and started preparing their dinner.

Catherine pulled a chair out from the dining table and sat down. Billy hovered over a sizzling frying pan. The familiar baritone voice of a national news anchor droned from the television, its volume set loud enough to overcome the sound of chicken browning. She said, "That smells wonderful."

"Thanks," he said. "The chicken is almost done. There's a salad in the fridge and a couple of potatoes in the microwave."

"You haven't left anything for me to do." Her smile told him she wasn't complaining.

"You fed me yesterday, and the day before." He kept half of his attention on the chicken and the other half tuned to the television, hoping to catch the stock market report.

She shrugged. "As I recall, you were wounded on both occasions."

"My sore butt didn't keep me from washing dishes last night. I should have offered to help sooner."

"If that chicken tastes as good as it smells, I won't care if you never wash another dish. Of the two of us, I think you are the better cook."

With a cocky grin, and a little bow, he said, "All us great chefs are considered artists in the kitchen."

"I'm not sure the title artist applies in this instance," Catherine replied. "After all, we are talking about a pan of homemade fried chicken, which smells wonderful, but isn't exactly five star restaurant fare."

"Do not mock my fried chicken, until you taste it."

"Okay, fair enough." Catherine flipped a few strands of damp hair off her face with a toss of her head, and returned his cocky grin with one of her own. "One wonders why your claim to artistry does not extend to sitting on a horse."

"Ouch!" He waved his cooking fork at her. "Be good, or I'll send you to bed without your supper."

He allowed his eyes to drift over her in a lazy way, making pink blossom in her cheeks. Her blond hair hung in unruly curls. Her freshly washed face glowed beneath some sort of cream that gave off the faint scent of roses. Without lipstick, her mouth blushed the same delicate shade as pink lemonade, and looked just as wholesome. Down at the lake, he'd tasted her lips more than once, but those kisses had left him thirsty and wanting to drink again.

The color of her cheeks deepened in response to the intimacy of his gaze. She fiddled with the lapels of her robe and pulled the belt tighter. Billy enjoyed knowing that he disturbed her.

"Tell you what," he said, flipping the chicken for the last time. "If you really want to help, you could set the table."

She raised one eyebrow and tapped a finger against her lips. "I suppose an Irish linen tablecloth and handmade beeswax candles are in order for your masterpiece."

"And soft music, something you could sing to," Billy teased. "I heard you singing in the shower." He chuckled.

"It's not my fault that I'm tone deaf," Catherine huffed and got to her feet. "I told you I'm the only one in my family with zero talent."

"There's something to be said for sheer volume," he mocked.

"Not nice, Caldwell." She laughed, then flounced over to the armoire, where she gathered an armful of clothing, before she disappeared into the tiny bathroom to dress.

"The potatoes will be done before long," he called after her.

When she returned, dressed in faded jeans and a blue flannel shirt, Billy didn't notice her. The television news seemed to be holding him spellbound. Puzzled, Catherine reached behind him and turned off the flame under the chicken. With the threat of a fire eliminated, she watched Billy watch the television program.

A female reporter, nearly breathless with excitement, was sharing a bit of local gossip with the viewers. The members of a top rock band had been attacked at a nightclub near Fisherman's Wharf in San Francisco. Film of a mob mauling one of the musicians accompanied the reporter's story. Catherine heard Billy swear under his breath.

"I wonder if he's all right?" Catherine sounded disgusted by the violence of the crowd. At her comment, Billy's head snapped around. When had she come back into the room? How much had she seen and heard? A sick feeling settled in the pit of his stomach. Moments ago, footage of him singing with the band had filled the television screen.

Catherine smiled at him. "I rescued your five star chicken. It was about to turn into charcoal chicken."

"Uh, thanks. Guess I got distracted." She wouldn't be smiling at him, if she had seen the damning part of the reporter's story. Billy sighed in relief, then sighed again in frustration. He worried that John might have been injured in the brawl.

After a moment's thought, he turned to Catherine. "You know, I think I should check to see if the Porsche got back safely."

"Good idea. Think how mad the owner would be if somebody stole his stolen car." She cocked her head and looked at him sideways.

Grinning, Billy picked up Catherine's cell phone and entered the number. "It's me. No, taking it easy, watching the news. Some rock star got his pretty clothes ripped. Probably served him right."

Rick laughed and agreed, letting Billy know that John had escaped the mob more or less undamaged.

Catherine began to set the table. In such close quarters, she couldn't help but listen to Billy's half of the phone conversation, but he didn't seem to mind. She reached for dishes in the cupboard, then took the potatoes out of the microwave.

"Not now," Billy responded to Rick's plea to return to the mansion. "And not if things stay the same. Put the big guy on, please."

A moment later, Carl growled in Billy's ear, "You got my baby all muddy."

Billy cleared his throat to keep from laughing. "Do I owe you for more than a headlight?"

Carl said, "Well, there's the bill for towing, and another for fixing the smashed light, and another for detailing, when the other stuff's done. Guess all those bills will go to the person responsible."

"Okay, I'm good for it," Billy said. "I thought I might have to pay for a whole new Porsche."

Six

Catherine fretted all through dinner. From what she had heard of Billy's phone call, he and his employer seemed to be back on good terms. She worried that he might return to his job at any moment, maybe as soon as tomorrow morning. The thought that he might leave before she had a chance to apologize cramped her stomach and turned the food on her plate to sawdust. But every time she tried to bring up their argument at the lake, Billy changed the subject. Frustrated and miserable, she rearranged the food on her plate, without eating any more of it. Instead, she watched Billy. He was gazing at the last piece of chicken on the platter.

"Do you want that?" she asked.

"The jury is still out," he replied, twirling his fork the way a drummer idly twirls a drumstick. "If I eat it now, I'll have eaten too much. If I wait a couple of minutes, it will disappear without a peep. Bad pun intended." He grinned at her.

"I'll keep you company, while you wait." She pushed her half-eaten supper out of the way and clasped her hands in front of her on the table.

"As long as you don't try to wash any of these dishes. Tonight, it's definitely my job." He waved his fork at her like a parent warning an unruly child to behave.

"That's fine. I've been wanting to talk to you, anyway." She found it hard to meet his eyes. Why was humbling yourself so darn difficult, even when you knew you were wrong? she wondered.

He sighed and shrugged. "Okay."

"I want to apologize for my behavior this afternoon."

When he would have interrupted her, she stopped him. "Please, listen."

He set his fork down on his plate and leaned back in his chair. "Go ahead."

"I've been acting like an idiot. I am so sorry."

"Apology accepted." He picked up his fork once more, speared the last piece of chicken, and dropped it on his plate.

Catherine frowned. Billy had forgiven her so easily, in such an offhand manner, he seemed disinterested. Her clasped hands began to shake. She said, "I need to explain. I need you to understand."

Billy glanced at her, then pushed his own plate out of the way, the rest of his supper forgotten. "Take your time."

"All my life…," Catherine paused to take a deep breath, then began again. "All my life I've felt like an outsider in my own family. I tried to fit in, but never could."

"Why?" Anxiety poured from her. Billy felt it like a third presence in the room.

"Both of my parents were consumed by their work, they still are consumed by their work. Always. I learned very early to stay silently in the background."

"What does that mean, exactly?"

"My mother and father solved the problem of parenthood by hiring a housekeeper. She was kind to us and kept us clean and fed. Sin and I learned not to expect attention from our parents, particularly not from our mother." A sheen of moisture gave false brightness to Catherine's eyes.

Catherine hadn't mentioned love. Billy concluded that she didn't expect love from her mother and father.

"Of course, things changed for Sin when they discovered his artistic genius. They created a space for him in my father's studio so he could spend all of his free time drawing and painting. So, he wasn't considered a nuisance." She looked down, hiding her expression.

"But you were a nuisance?" Billy felt his jaw begin to tighten.

"That's probably not the right word to describe my place in the family. Invisible might be a more accurate description."

"So, you weren't constantly underfoot, or calling attention to yourself."

"No, not very often. Sometimes I did try to fit in." She wore a sad smile that said more than she had said about her efforts, and the response they got from her parents. "I was like a penguin trying to soar with eagles. Knowing that you can't fly doesn't always keep your feet on the ground."

"I'm amazed that you and your brother are close, the way your parents favored him."

Catherine shrugged. "Actually, they were more his mentors than his parents."

"What did you do while the three famous artists communed with their muses?" His question sounded snide, and he meant it to be.

"I posed for a lot of paintings. One by my father, Girl With Violets, is quite well-known. Then I discovered horses. I told my parents that I wanted to learn to ride and they signed me up for lessons. When I wasn't in school, I spent all of my time hanging around the stable."

"And I bet it never occurred to them that a stable could be a dangerous place for a little kid without supervision." Billy's outrage grew with each new disclosure.

"They would have approved of anything that got me out of the house. Luckily, I didn't get hurt and, in the end, I benefitted. I got to spend most of my time with a horse trainer."

"So, you found an adult who did take an interest in you?"

"Yes. He gave me a lot of encouragement, taught me about his job and everything about horses. He entered me in riding competitions, and celebrated with me when I won. Still, our friendship, as close as it became over the years, didn't make up for what I was missing at home. I kept trying to impress my parents by doing a lot of stuff for them."

Billy suspected that he knew the answer, before he asked, "What about the housekeeper?" "Long gone. They fired her once Sin and I could fix simple meals for ourselves. They said another adult living in the house intruded on their privacy."

"Made them feel guilty, you mean," Billy corrected her.

Catherine looked startled for a moment, then thoughtful as she considered his suggestion. "Maybe. By the time I turned fourteen, I had taken over nearly all of the daily decision making. You've met my mother, so you can see why I did it."

"To keep the peace."

"I've always been very good at organization. Compared to them, I was the genius. After my eighteenth birthday, they started paying me a salary."

"Damn, they were using you!" If her parents had been there, he would have kicked their butts.

"It took me years to figure out that they didn't care if tax forms were filed correctly, or bills paid on time. My job was booking airline tickets and hiring limousines, theirs was to climb aboard and go."

Billy shook his head in disgust. "So you made their carefree lifestyle work for them, but it didn't work for you?"

Catherine nodded. "My need for approval kept running headlong into reality."

"How so?"

"At first, I made an easy target for people who wanted to get close to my parents. Most teenage girls don't receive loads of flattery."

"So you started to mistrust people." Billy stated, matter-of-factly. He'd understood that about her already.

"I never knew if I was liked for myself, or for what I could do to influence my parents."

Billy smiled. "The clever ones would bring a chunk of meat to bribe the lioness guarding the gate. But, in your case, instead of an antelope haunch, something they thought you'd fall for."

She chuckled, and smiled back at him. "I enjoyed the flowers, and I ate some of the candy, but I always refused the jewelry."

"Smart girl!"

Suddenly, the smile left her face. She shoved her chair back from the table and stood. "I can't let you think that my parents were monsters. They weren't."

He looked up at her. "No, just very, very self-centered. People don't have to be evil to hurt others. Sometimes they only have to look the other way."

"What do you mean?"

"I think your parents were so caught up in the hype of being celebrities, either they didn't notice your unhappiness, or they didn't realize its depth. I'll bet, if you asked them today, they would say that you had a wonderful childhood."

Catherine began to pace the length of the room. "A lot of it was happy. Sin and I got to travel all over the world. We got to do things other kids only dream about."

"Which makes me wonder where in the world your brother was while you were doing everything you could to make life easy for your mother and father." Billy believed that brothers ought to protect their sisters. He intended to talk to her brother about that.

"Some of the time he went to a boarding school in Ireland. Sin loved it there."

That piece of information added to Billy's anger toward Catherine's parents. "Why didn't you get to go away to school? Were you too useful to be allowed to escape?"

Catherine stopped pacing and faced him. "I didn't want to go anywhere. I loved my time at the stable. And I kept hoping things at home would change as I got older and proved to my parents just how well I managed their business arrangements."

Billy had never been so close to ramming his fist through a wall. To his way of thinking, Catherine's mother and father were a prime pair of losers.

He got to his feet and stepped around the table to stand beside her. "I watched the way you managed your mother this morning. That kid who always sacrificed herself for others no longer exists." He took her hand and she let him.

"My parents will never be satisfied. A few months ago I stopped trying to please them. What I can't figure out is why you put up with me."

"Guess."

She gazed up at him as if trying to read his thoughts "I have no idea."

He smiled and swept her up into his arms. In four long strides he reached the bed and settled into the pillows with her cuddled beside him. He smiled a different sort of smile and said, "The first time you were in my arms, you went to my head."

"I did?" Her eyes went wide in surprise.

Billy thought the joy on her face was the kind reserved for a child's first glimpse of a rainbow, full of innocent wonder. Catherine was innocent in a lot of ways, he reminded himself.

He held her in the crook of his arm so he could nibble at her astonished mouth. He kissed her, lightly at first, then deeper. He tasted the little plateau where her cheek met her ear, then traced the edge of her ear with his tongue. He blew gently, drying the moisture left by his caress, and made her shiver. She sighed.

He swept the tangled hair away from her face. He stroked his fingers through the strands, smoothing them. He bent to her and skimmed his lips over her forehead, pausing to plant a kiss above each brow, and another on the bridge of her nose. She made a soft sound as he dropped tender kisses on her eyelids. He framed her face with his hands and covered her mouth with his. Holding her close, he indulged her curiosity about sex with a second, exquisitely frustrating lesson.

Lucky moved easily beneath her, for once following her commands instead of resisting them. Catherine smiled as the horse trotted over a series of crossed poles raised a few inches off the ground. Progress! She reined him around in a tight circle and aimed him at the poles once again. Lucky's ears pricked forward showing his interest in this new game. He hopped over the little jumps as lightly as a white tailed fawn bounding across a meadow. She stroked Lucky's gleaming neck and lavished him with praise.

It was a delicious day. The best day of her life. She'd spent the night in the arms of the man she loved. Well, almost. They had shared her bed, but she had slept between the sheets while Billy lay on top of the quilt. The sleeping arrangements were a compromise. Billy had been adamant, "No sex!" He'd said he didn't want to wake up the next morning thinking he had taken advantage of her. When he made love to her, he had said, he wanted it to be perfect. Not after an emotional conversation about neglectful parents. That wasn't his idea of courtship. That was the word he had used. "Courtship." It was a word with a future.

Out of sheer exuberance, Catherine touched her heels to the colt's sides and urged him into a gallop. Lucky sensed her excitement and put his heart into it. He raced around the perimeter of the arena, hooves pounding thunder, mane and tail streaming in the wind. Catherine shouted for joy.

The day sped by. Catherine's good spirits lasted all morning, even after her brother arrived during lunch and dragged Billy off to the studio, saying he needed her handyman's help with his latest project. She supposed Sin wanted to move another piece of heavy furniture into the studio. Billy looked a bit sullen. He tossed the remains of his sandwich onto his plate and seemed reluctant as he trailed behind her brother over to the old house.

After she finished her meal, she returned to the arena, this time riding the stallion named Admiral. She always schooled the powerful animal in the afternoon, after he'd had plenty of time to work off his excess energy out in the unconfined space of the meadow. Today, the stallion was in an unusually good mood. Maybe her own buoyant spirits had spilled over onto all of her horses. It seemed that falling in love had produced extraordinary and unexpected benefits.

She laughed, loving being in love, as she guided the stallion toward a pair of jumps spaced close together. The jumps weren't particularly tall considering the ability of the horse she rode, only about five feet high. He could clear a seven foot fence with lots of room to spare. As they raced toward the first of the two fences, she felt Admiral gather himself, preparing to leap over it. His ears were forward, attention focused, ready.

A car roared up the driveway, its horn blaring. The stallion swerved, throwing both horse and rider off balance and in danger of crashing into the first jump. Admiral gave a tremendous lunge and leaped straight up and over it.

Catherine toppled backwards out of the saddle, hitting the ground with a bone-jarring thud that left her ears ringing and her lungs without air. She lay on her back on the sandy floor of the arena, gasping for breath.

Though it defied logic, it seemed only seconds before Billy and her brother fell to their knees at her side. The two barraged her with worried questions she couldn't answer. She flapped her hands at them, trying to move them out of her way. Then, ever so slowly, she rolled onto her side and took a shallow breath.

"I'm...okay..." She forced the words out as she struggled to sit up. She twisted her shoulders and shook off the two panic-stricken men who were doing more to hinder her than to help her. Finally, she drew in a huge breath of air and filled her lungs. Relief was immediate.

"Shouldn't you lie down, until the ambulance comes?" Billy fretted.

"Oh, no!" she cried, "Tell me you didn't call for the paramedics." She imagined being surrounded by even more worried faces, and started to laugh. "I'm fine. Really. I just got the wind knocked out of me for a moment. For heaven's sake, call them back and tell them it's a false alarm!"

Catherine felt more embarrassed than anything else. She hadn't fallen off a horse in years. Whenever she rode, she was always alert and ready for anything. Of course, no one could be ready for some micro-brained jackass barreling up the driveway with a hand glued to the car's horn.

She aimed a killing look at the stranger standing just outside the arena fence and scrambled to her feet.

The huge man stood nearly seven feet tall. The top rail of the fence cut across his bulky form at the exact level where his neck thrust down between his wide shoulders and disappeared into his massive chest. Through the lower bars of the fence, his legs looked like tree trunks. Under his jacket, he wore a silky red shirt open down the front, revealing an impressive chest covered in tight black curls. His skin shown rich as polished ebony. Around his neck he wore a heavy gold chain that would have made King Tut jealous.

Catherine was not impressed. She turned her back on the intruder and walked around the jump to take control of the frightened stallion.

Admiral's sides were heaving and patches of sweat stood out on his sides and chest. His eyes rolled and showed white as Catherine came near. She held out her hand and his nostrils flared as he drew in her familiar scent. After a moment, she stepped forward and gathered up the dangling reins. She ran a hand along Admiral's cheek, murmuring reassurances. The stallion rammed his head into her chest in a horsy greeting and she chuckled.

"Nice jump, sweetheart," she crooned, "next time, how about taking me with you?"

Catherine glanced over her shoulder. Billy had confronted the stranger. The men's body language screamed tension. In contrast, their voices were pitched too low for her to hear. Billy appeared to be taking the stranger to task for his thoughtlessness. A day earlier, Catherine would have bristled at Billy's interference, and would have insisted on speaking for herself. After last night, after sleeping nestled in his arms, it seemed right that a man should defend his woman. Even so, she wanted to add a few choice words of her own to his. She tugged on Admiral's reins and moved toward the two men. Her brother joined her, tagging along behind the stallion, just out of kicking range of its hooves.

As the little parade approached, it became clear to Catherine that an argument raged across a battle line drawn at the fence. She came close enough to catch Billy's whispered, "So, get the hell out of here!"

The stranger on the other side of the fence looked at her curiously. She stood a few feet behind Billy, holding the stallion's reins in one hand, while she met that interested stare with one of her own. For a moment, she wondered why two men whose anger seemed so obvious had been doing battle in whispers. Then realization knotted her stomach. Billy hadn't heard her step up behind him and didn't know she was standing there. He wasn't a man defending his woman, he was a man hiding something from her.

Catherine's puzzlement turned to suspicion, then to anger. She clenched her fists and ordered herself to remain calm.

"No way, man," the stranger said, his eyes steady on her face. "You can't expect us just to cool our heels until you're ready." The man's voice rumbled, pitched very low, and Catherine concluded that a deep bass was the giant's normal tone.

Before Billy could respond, Sin cleared his throat loudly.

Catherine spun toward her brother. She knew a fake cough when she heard one. For some reason, Sin had warned Billy that she was near enough to hear what was being said.

Billy turned and gaped at her. His face grew red. He swallowed hard several times. She could almost see the wheels turning in his brain, assessing, guessing, wondering when she had slipped up behind him, and wondering what she might have heard. "Say," the overly bright words spilled forth like trinkets from a shoplifter's pocket, "don't you think you should walk Admiral around to cool him off? He looks pretty sweaty to me."

"Oh, I don't think so. Why don't you introduce me to your friend?" Her reply, quiet and pleasant, masked emotions too intense and tangled for her to unravel. But fury outweighed all of the rest.

The stranger chimed in, an odd expression on his face. "Yeah, Billy, why don't you introduce me to the lady?"

"That won't be necessary, since you are leaving immediately." Billy's reply hovered just short of a threat.

Catherine's eyes skimmed from one man to the other. A hint of a smile curled the corners of the stranger's mouth. From Billy's rigid posture, she could tell that he had just become the focus of some sort of mischief. Out of the corner of her eye, she could see her brother leaning against the arena fence. Sin wore an aura of expectancy that annoyed her.

Her brother was a keen observer of other people, so impersonal sometimes that he seemed not to have ordinary human emotions. Catherine didn't care for that habit, particularly when he aimed his detached gaze in her direction. Moreover, she didn't approve, because those who did not know Sin well had been hurt by his aloof behavior. And now, she was being dragged into some sort of drama. Whether she played a bit part, or became the star of the show, her brother would offer her no help. The next act in the play was up to her.

"Since Billy is being so rude," she said, leading the horse closer to the two men, "perhaps we should introduce ourselves?" Never let it be said that Catherine Anne O'Shea acted like a coward, she thought. She shot her brother a defiant look. Sin raised one questioning eyebrow and continued to watch the scene unfold.

"No!" Billy stepped in front of Catherine. With the stallion beginning to tug nervously at the reins, she couldn't make her way around him.

"I'm through taking orders, Billy," the big man rumbled. "I thought we cleared that up a few days ago. Cherokee is a partnership."

Billy's features were stark with emotion. The look he gave Catherine pleaded for patience, for understanding of events that seemed to her beyond understanding. Her body felt suddenly hollow as all of her earlier happiness drained away. The first tendrils of despair began to grow somewhere near her heart. She shuddered.

Billy turned back to the man standing on the opposite side of the fence. "We didn't clear up anything! You and John want to play games with groupies and I want to play music. I'm not coming back, so save your breath."

"I'm not here to argue, dammit!" One enormous fist slammed onto the fence, coming close to breaking the top rail.

Billy remained unmoved. "I'm not in the mood for more of your bull."

"Just listen, okay?" Two huge hands gripped the fence. "After you phoned, and we realized you weren't coming back, well, I guess we figured out that you might have been right about a few things. So, we traced you through caller ID. I thought I should come talk to you."

"What's going on here?" Catherine's voice shook as she took hold of Billy's arm.

"Please, sweetheart, it's just a disagreement that Carl and I have to work out. Nothing to concern you." He patted the hand that held his arm.

Catherine's patience with the situation hit zero. No one, not even the man she loved, dismissed her like a child too stupid to understand what the adults were talking about. She took another step forward and pushed Billy aside. The jittery horse behind her gave her additional authority.

"Carl? That's your name, right?" The big man nodded, and the final pieces of the puzzle fell into place as she recalled what Billy had said about the owner of the Porsche.

In perfect French, she said, "Well, Carl, since you are on my property, why don't you tell me what propelled you and your little rocket ship up my driveway?" She smiled and gestured with a tilt of her head toward the black Porsche parked near the arena. Then she leveled a murderous look at Billy and added in English, "It's one of six, so I'm told."

Carl, mistaking the pleasant tone of her voice, launched into an explanation. "Yeah, that's right. I was pretty mad when Billy took off in it." He turned to bestow a fond glance on the pricey machine. "It's my favorite, had it the longest."

"I see," Catherine said, "like favoring your firstborn child." The smile she turned on the unsuspecting man glowed brilliant as a second sun. Sin snickered and boosted himself up to sit somewhat unsteadily on the fence close to Carl.

"Catherine..." Billy began.

She turned back to her new acquaintance with another benevolent smile. Carl frowned and darted a glance at Billy. She glanced at Billy as well, saying, "I'm sure Carl has lots of interesting things he can tell me about you, darling. Don't you agree?"

When Billy would have answered, she hushed him. "No, let Carl speak. I'm dying to hear what he has to say." She paused, then prompted, "Please, go on, Carl."

The big man began to look uncomfortable. "Well, I was still kinda mad later that evening. But, when Billy didn't come back to the mansion, we all got really worried."

"Yes, back to the mansion. I sympathize. How distressing it must have been for the three of you. It is three, right?"

She waited for a response. Billy, Carl, and even Sin, nodded like crime scene witnesses too stunned to do anything but tell the truth. She went on, "The three of you waiting through a seemingly endless night."

Carl nodded. "Yeah, we didn't get much sleep."

"I'm sure," Catherine commented in a tone as dry as California's Anza-Borrego Desert. "We all tend to become quite upset, when someone we know suddenly disappears, don't we? Especially if that someone is as, could we say, extraordinary as William Caldwell?"

She turned to Billy and inquired, "You are known these days by some other name, I believe?"

Before Billy could respond, she continued, "What happened next, Carl? I'm absolutely fascinated by your story."

"Uh, maybe I should leave?" Carl started to back away from the fence.

Billy spoke before Catherine could. "No, it's too late now." His voice sounded strained, he seemed resigned to endure whatever might follow. "Answer her questions. All of her questions." He turned and walked off across the arena.

"Carl, you just don't look like a carpenter to me. What is it that you do?" Catherine struggled to appear composed. Her fingers had gone numb where she clutched Admiral's woven leather reins.

"I play keyboard. Write a few lyrics. You know."

"No, Carl, I do not know. I need you to tell me." She looked at Billy standing near one of the jumps and felt almost sorry for him. Then she allowed her anger to surge and wash away all traces of sympathy. He had lied to her. More than once. And now, she would find out the truth.

"What is Billy's job?"

"Let's see. He does lots of stuff for Cherokee. Lead singer, composer, writes most of the lyrics, arranges the music. Lots of stuff. He takes care of the business end, too. You know, contracts and concert dates, and such."

"So, he's very smart. Would you say that's true?"

"Oh, sure. Billy's real bright."

"Then, he would know when he'd overstayed his welcome, wouldn't he?"

"Well, sure." Carl glanced at Billy's lone form, then down at the slim woman in front of him. He could see the effort it took for her to appear self-contained. "I'm sorry," he said.

"It's not your fault," she said as tears threatened.

"You want me to slug him for you?" Carl asked.

Catherine swiped at a tear that clung to her lashes and managed a small smile. "No, thanks. I'm learning to fight my own battles."

"Good for you, Sis!" Sin swung down from the fence and attempted to give her a hug. She slid out from under her brother's embrace and moved away, leaving him staring at the back end of a huge, black horse.

"You knew who he was all along!" She accused, tossing the words over her shoulder, as she marched across the arena to confront the stranger she had hired as her handyman. "Don't bother to deny it, Sin. It explains all that smirking you did when I introduced you. You must have found the whole thing very amusing. Your clueless sister hires a world famous rock star to muck out her barn. Hilarious."

Billy leaned against the artificial red blocks of a jump that looked like a section of brick wall. He'd loosed his long hair and it lifted in the light breeze, framing his strong features like black wings. His arms were crossed over his chest, making him look for all the world like a man relaxing in the sunshine. Only the muscles bunching in his jaw revealed his agitation.

"You lied to me," Catherine said. She was surprised by the reasonable tone of her voice.

"Never." His response was equally calm. The confrontation that he had feared was upon him, but unlike anything he had imagined. It wasn't a flaming row. Catherine stood before him, cold and flat as an arctic ice floe, her face and voice without expression. That same cold gripped Billy's heart. He felt helpless to change a single detail of the scene. He dropped his arms to his sides and took a step toward her.

Catherine took a step back. "I'm not a fool. Weird upbringing and all, even I know that the lead singer of Cherokee is named Billy Raven." Tears began to spill, hot against her bloodless cheeks.

Seeing her cry hurt worse than torture, but Billy didn't know what to say to stop her tears. "William Raven Caldwell. I didn't lie to you."

"Oh, no, not in words. Not technically." She shook her head in denial. "What a good lawyer you would have been!" Bitterness tinged her voice.

"Catherine, I love you." He heard his own desperation. The pledge, meant to be a prayer for forgiveness, came out all wrong.

Catherine didn't think it was possible to hurt more than she did already, but his words brought agony. She had to strike back. "I'm so happy to hear that. Oh, yes! A complete stranger is in love with me. How wonderful."

"Dammit, Catherine, what was I supposed to say?" He stretched a hand toward her, imploring. "If I had told you who I was, you wouldn't have given me the time of day."

She wanted to slap his hand away. Instead, she took another step back. "So, now it's my fault? You lie, and it's my fault? I don't think so!"

She had to escape, before pain and anger destroyed her. She turned in one quick motion and pulled the stallion's reins up over his head as she leaped into the saddle. Blinded by tears, she thrust her heels into Admiral's sides. The stallion bolted toward the open meadow. Admiral didn't seem to care that the arena fence stood between him and freedom. Neither did Catherine.

She heard Billy shout for her to stop, but there would be no stopping. Not now, not ever.

She felt Admiral gather himself for the leap.

Seven

Catherine's phone rang that afternoon. She looked at the caller's number and frowned. The first time he called, she didn't recognize the number. There was no other identification. She didn't feel like talking to anyone, so she didn't answer. Sunk in misery, she thought about turning off her phone, but couldn't, in case a client wanted to speak to her. After that first call, her phone rang several different times during the rest of the day. Always the same number, always unanswered. The caller's persistence told Catherine who it was. Billy Raven. Not content to break her heart, now it seemed that he was trying to break her spirit. Or whatever was left of it, after she jumped Admiral over the arena fence and galloped as far away as she could get.

Billy didn't give up. He tried again the next day. Catherine thought about canceling her mobile service. When she inquired about doing that, her hopes were dashed by the enormous cancellation fee that she would be charged for breaking her contract. So her phone rang and she refused to answer. And every time it rang she remembered how it felt to be betrayed.

Her brother was no better. He called and called and called. Finally, he must have figured out that she had no intention to speak to him. The calls stopped. Just in case he tried to confront her in person, Catherine locked the iron gate to block the driveway. If Sin came there, he would get the message. He was no longer welcome on Hidden Lake Farm.

Finally, her phone fell silent.

Catherine forced herself out of bed. She forced herself to feed the horses. She forced herself to clean their stalls. She forced herself to ride each horse as she always had done.

She plodded through the grey winter day and fell into bed without feeling she had done her best. She knew she hadn't, but didn't seem to care.

Sleep came in fits and starts, and was never restful. When Catherine remembered that she hadn't shopped for food since she locked the front gate, she realized that she hadn't been eating much for the past couple of days. She looked in the mirror at the dark circles under her eyes and at her disheveled hair, and felt frightened.

Catherine took a shower, washed her hair, changed into clean clothes, and went shopping. At the supermarket, nothing looked good. The thought of cooking a meal seemed overwhelming. Her mind emptied when she tried to remember what went into a balanced diet. After wandering aimlessly around the store, she chose a loaf of bread, some apples, and three cans of tuna. She added a bottle of daily vitamins. Then she went back for a half-gallon of milk. Exhausted, she paid for her groceries and drove back to the farm. There, she drank a glass of milk and took a nap.

When she woke an hour later, she gazed into the mirror a second time. It didn't take a PhD in psychology to figure out what was wrong with her. Anger and heartache haunted her thoughts. Everywhere she looked on the farm there were reminders of Billy the rock star pretending to be William the carpenter. Anger and heartache were turning her into a stranger to herself. Anger and heartache were bad for business, and threatened all that she had worked so hard to achieve.

In the barn, a shaft of pale sunlight that sparkled as it fell from the window William had repaired brought her no pleasure. She resisted an urge to break the window again. Instead, she erased as many signs of his three days on the farm as she could. She removed the chair he had used from beside her kitchen table and stored it away in an empty stall. She folded the blanket he wrapped around himself that first night and left it on the seat of the abandoned chair. She poured the last of the sherry down the drain and threw the bottle into the trash, along with the coffee mug he had used. She stuffed the quilt Billy slept on during their last night together into a large trash bag and pushed it out of sight under her bed.

There was nothing she could do to remove traces of him from Sin's studio in the old house, other than never going there again. The rest, like the repairs he made to the barn's leaky roof, she would have to accept, and then get on with her life. She plunged into work on the farm.

Every time she began to think of Billy, of his winning grin, of her hands tangled in his mane of long black hair, of the tempting scent of his neck when he held her in his arms, she ruthlessly thought of something else. Her mood didn't improve by much, but she learned that she didn't need to be happy, or content, to keep her training stable running.

On the second Saturday of each month, Catherine gave horsemanship lessons to young children to supplement her income. The six little girls who had signed up for classes were full of energy. With her life in ruins, Catherine dreaded the added pressure of conducting the lesson, but she couldn't cancel at the last minute.

When pickup trucks pulling trailers began to arrive, she stood beside the driveway, ready to help unload the children's horses. Soon the driveway was crowded and chaotic. The little girls, who were eight and nine years old, shouted and giggled and hugged their horses around their necks. Each girl was required to bridle and saddle her own mount. The two youngest girls had to stand on empty wooden crates to accomplish the task. Always polite, Catherine shooed overly helpful parents out of the way.

Once the horses were saddled and bridled, Catherine checked the children's efforts, praising and adjusting and tightening girths. "Okay," she called, "time to mount up."

Six little monkeys climbed into their saddles and waited for her instructions. The girls were not particularly quiet, shouting to one another and giggling, but their horses were well behaved and tolerant.

"Single file, now, ladies. Anita, you lead the way into the arena."

Being called ladies made the girls laugh.

Anita, all seriousness, said, "Yes, Miss O'Shea." She turned her pinto toward the arena and set off at a trot.

"Not so fast, Anita!" Catherine called after her. "Wait for the others to catch up." The girl pulled her horse to a stop. A ragged line of riders formed behind her pinto.

Catherine said, "Walk on," and the group moved into the arena at a sedate pace. The girls lined their horses up side by side in the center of a large open space away from the jump course.

Catherine began the lesson with a review of last month's homework. "Who can tell me the parts of an English saddle?" Six hands shot up, and two girls shouted, "Me, me!"

"How about each of you naming one part?" Catherine suggested.

Anita shouted, "Stirrups!"

Lauren complained, "That's what I was going to say."

"Choose another," Catherine said.

"Okay, pommel."

"Right." Catherine pointed to Beth, "You're next." Beth thought for a moment, bounced up and down, and said, "Seat."

Rosalie watched Beth bounce on her horse's back and shouted, "Gullet, so the saddle doesn't hurt the horse's back."

Sarah didn't wait to be asked. "Girth, so the saddle doesn't fall off."

All the girls laughed.

Monica was last to answer. "Stirrup leathers," she said, grinning hugely, "so the stirrups don't fall off."

There was more laughter, and six smiling faces turned toward Catherine. "I can see," she said, "that all of you spent a lot of time on your homework. Good work, girls!"

As the lesson progressed, Catherine took her students through the basics of riding, starting with walking on, whoa, and walking on again. She had the girls change direction at a walk, then at a trot. They took turns riding their horses over tiny jumps. As a reward for following her instructions, she allowed the girls to canter their horses several times around the arena. The rocking chair motion was the girls' favorite gait, and, besides, the faster pace was exciting. Beginning riders at Hidden Lake Farm were not allowed to gallop their horses. Catherine was very strict about that.

Near the end of the lesson, Catherine asked the girls to dismount and lead their horses around the arena to cool them down. Back on the driveway, the girls stripped the tack from their mounts, brushed them, buckled them into their blankets, and loaded them into the trailers. The lesson was over, except for assigning homework.

Catherine said, "Since you did so well on the parts of an English saddle, for next month's lesson, please learn the parts of a horse. There are a lot more parts to a horse than heads and tails and hooves."

Monica smirked and said, "Ears."

Monica's mother gave her a stern look and said, "Nobody likes a smarty pants."

As the pickups pulling trailers began lining up on the driveway to leave, Catherine escaped into the silence of her apartment. There, with shaking hands, she filled a glass with water. Pretending to be cheerful had been harder than she expected.

She knew she should feel proud of herself, because not a single little girl, or any of their parents, saw through her happy facade to the heartbreak underneath. That gave her hope. She could go on working with the horses in her stable, and give progress reports to their owners, without breaking down in front of them. She imagined the reaction she would get from a tear-stained face and puffy eyes.

It would be impossible to explain, impossible to tell the truth, impossible to avoid their questions and their offers of sympathy. Or, maybe, if she did tell them the truth, they would criticize her for being stupid and falling in love with an imposter.

Catherine choked back a sob. She would not cry over Billy Raven this morning. She would do her best to put him out of her mind, at least during working hours. In the evening, with no one to witness her misery, she could cry all she wanted. She would wait.

She drank the rest of the water, left the glass in the sink, and turned toward the back door. Now that the riding lesson was over, she planned to drive to the feed store and place an order. She wasn't hungry these days, but she couldn't say the same for the horses. She grabbed her purse, gave herself a quick check in the mirror by the door, and stepped out into the stable yard. In less than a minute, she was in her battered pickup headed for the gate.

As her truck rounded the corner of the barn onto the driveway, Catherine repeated a few swear words she had picked up from Sin, and stomped on the brake. A dark green truck towing a trailer blocked her way. Lauren's father, looking relaxed in a studied way, leaned against the side of his truck. Lauren, obviously uncomfortable, shuffled her feet in the weeds growing beside the driveway. The girl shot Catherine a helpless glance and looked toward her father. Catherine felt her teeth clench. She pasted a pleasant smile on her face and climbed from her pickup.

"Mr. Landry." She walked up to the man. "Is there something that I can do for you?"

Tall and slim and blond, the man was handsome, and acted as if he knew it. There was an arrogance about him that she hadn't seen in a man since she left her mother's employment. Shallow, self-involved men had been the rule among her mother's acquaintances and business connections, the people Catherine had dealt with on a daily basis. Besides being predictable and boring, their arrogance hid a kind of neediness that was the source of constant demands for attention. Men like that had always rubbed her the wrong way, and this man was no exception.

Catherine's well-practiced smile straightened to a tight line.

Landry didn't seem to notice. He turned his interested attention on her. His eyes traveled over her in a way that felt like an invasion of privacy. The smile that followed his inspection failed to convey good humor, but pretended that it did. "Yes, there is something you can do. You can call me Doug."

Lauren slid behind her father's truck out of sight. Catherine watched the girl disappear with a sinking feeling in the pit of her stomach.

"Mr. Landry," Catherine insisted upon calling him by his last name, "what can I help you with?"

"Miss O'Shea," he replied, his tone just short of mocking, "we have known each other for three months, now. I think it's time to drop the formality in favor of first names."

Catherine shook her head. "An hour or so each month spent watching your daughter ride her horse is not a friendship."

His grin widened. "Then we should get to know each other better, shouldn't we? Ask me anything, and I will tell you all about myself."

Catherine believed that, without a doubt, Landry was his own most ardent fan.

"What do you want to know?" he asked, undaunted by her lack of enthusiasm.

Catherine swallowed the first comment that came to mind. She might lose him as a client, if she asked him when he planned on leaving. She lied and said, "I can't think of a single thing."

At that moment, Lauren popped up from her hiding place and said, "Dad, I have to go."

He replied to the girl, without taking his eyes from Catherine. "We'll go in a little while."

"No," Lauren insisted, "I have to go, now!"

Catherine said, "I think she needs to use the restroom." Lauren nodded vigorously. "I'll take her."

Catherine took Lauren's hand and led her into the barn.

"The restroom is over there," she said, pointing to her tiny lavatory. Lauren hurried off, leaving Catherine alone with her thoughts. Lauren's father was a jerk. She would have to speak with him in a way that didn't embarrass Lauren, but was firm enough for him to get the message that she wasn't interested in him. She'd had plenty of practice with that sort of thing in her past life. She knew that she could handle Mr. Landry. Still, she resented the added stress that he was causing her. With a shake of her head, Catherine reminded herself not to let her resentment show, and to be polite at all costs.

Dealing with him was just one more reason why she wished she could curl up in her bed and miss living through the rest of the afternoon. She needed sleep, but she knew that she wasn't likely to get any. For the past few days, whenever she tried to sleep, dreams of Billy set her heart racing, and she woke with a start, knowing that she wouldn't fall asleep again. Each time sleep eluded her, she dragged herself out of bed, drank a cup of coffee, and wished she could find something useful to do, even at four o'clock in the morning. With so little energy and so little incentive, she surrendered to her insomnia and sat at her kitchen table, doing nothing.

"Miss O'Shea?" Lauren had returned without Catherine noticing.

"Miss O'Shea," the girl repeated. "I really love horses."

"Yes, I can see that you do. You take very good care of Princess."

"She is my best friend. I love brushing her and feeding her and, and, just everything."

Catherine gazed at Lauren and saw herself in the little girl. Loving horses had been her own escape from unhappiness. Still, she didn't know anything about Lauren's circumstances. There could be a lot of reasons for the girl to be horse crazy. Lots of girls her age went through a stage where horses consumed their thoughts. They took riding lessons, drew pictures of horses, wore riding boots everywhere they went, and just plain loved horses, no matter what. Most of the time, the love affair lasted until the girls discovered boys. At that point, quite a few horses changed owners, and different little girls had their fondest dreams come true on their birthdays, or at Christmas. And sometimes, a girl like Lauren became an excellent rider and won lots of ribbons in the show ring. There was no predicting.

Catherine said, "Princess is a very lucky horse. I'm sure she would tell you how much she loves you, if she could."

"Oh, I know she does! "

"Well, then, let's go talk to your father, so Princess can get out of her trailer and have more fun with you back home."

Lauren dashed ahead, while Catherine followed more slowly.

Landry wasn't standing beside his truck. Catherine groaned and asked the empty air, "What now?"

Then Lauren spotted her father, and ran toward the old house. He stood on the porch, peering in the windows that looked out onto the front yard. As he moved from one window to the next, Landry gave the decrepit swing a push. The rusted chains groaned loudly enough for Catherine to hear yards away on the driveway. She realized that she would have to hurry and stop the pair, before their explorations pushed through the front door into the house itself. Thanks to William the carpenter's recent repairs, the heavy door opened easily, now.

Catherine sped after Lauren, intent on controlling the situation.

Lauren hopped up the porch steps. Landry greeted his daughter with a brief one-arm hug. "Well, you took your time, didn't you?"

"Miss O'Shea and I were talking about horses."

"I see," he said. His eyes were aimed over Lauren's head while he watched Catherine jog toward the porch.

Catherine came to a stop on the bottom step. She didn't want to encourage the man by joining him up on the porch. Not that it seemed that he needed any encouragement. "This is an interesting old place," he said. "I wonder, is it filled with antiques?"

Catherine imagined him poking through the contents of the house, ripping off dust covers and opening drawers. She imagined him as a cat burglar, casing the place before he snuck back during the night and stole everything of value. She wasn't being exactly fair in her judgment of him, but he was pushing the limits of her patience. She stared at him, until he looked away. She said, "No antiques. Just my landlady's furniture that she plans to pick up, once she is settled in a new house." This last was a complete fabrication and had nothing to do with her landlady's plans for the farm.

He smiled. "Too bad."

"Not really," Catherine replied. "However, I'm sure that she would object to strangers looking around her property without her permission."

Lauren had the good sense to tug on her father's hand, and say, "Let's go, Daddy."

Landry, his face cut by another annoying smile, moved toward the steps. Catherine turned and started down the path that led through the weed-choked front yard to the driveway. The treasure hunter and his daughter followed after her.

Back beside his truck, he said, "Actually, I didn't intend to intrude on your landlady's privacy." Another innocent smile did nothing to deflect Catherine's pointed response.

"What did you intend?" she asked.

"Only to kill time, until you came back. With Lauren, of course."

"Yes, with Lauren." She gazed at the man, waiting for his next irritating comment.

"Could we walk a bit?" He looked off toward the meadow where the wind was ruffling dry winter grass that hadn't been cropped by the horses.

Catherine shook her head. "No, I don't have the time."

"Well, I was hoping to speak to you without Lauren listening in."

Now, Catherine smiled. "Perhaps you should have phoned, instead."

Looking a little less sure of himself, he said, "Maybe... Yeah, maybe you're right."

"So?" She let the question drag out, waiting to see what he would do next. He reminded her so much of one of her mother's sycophants, she felt she had entered a rift in time that had tumbled her backward into years past. She might be wearing dusty jeans and boots instead of a designer suit, but the conversation was eerily the same. She might grow old waiting for him to get to the point.

Still, he stood there expecting some signal from her that would allow him to proceed. She wouldn't give it to him.

"Okay, okay," he said, at last. "This meeting is not going the way I envisioned it."

Catherine focused on the word meeting. Suddenly, the conversation had something to do with business. That didn't make much sense to her. There was nothing about her business that she thought she needed to discuss with him. So it must be something about his business. She tried unsuccessfully to remember what Landry did for a living. He looked like a professional golfer, with a lithe build, but there was a softness about him that told her he wasn't an athlete. With that ready smile, she decided he had to be a salesman of some sort.

"How should this meeting go?" she asked.

He sighed. "Better. More friendly. Not so distantly polite."

Catherine nodded. He was more perceptive than she had given him credit for. "I think you should say what you came to say."

"Yes. You're right, again. Sometimes the direct approach is the right one." He looked at his daughter who stood listening to every word, and shrugged.

"I agree," Catherine said.

"I wanted to ask you out," he said. "I am asking you out. For next Friday."

"Next Friday?"

"Yeah, Valentine's Day. There's a party at my office. Champagne, the works. Best caterer in town." He grinned.

Catherine was stunned. She stood speechless for a moment, as she considered how inappropriate the invitation was. The holiday for lovers as a first date? The man wasn't just full of himself, he was living in a fantasy world where all his desires were fulfilled just by smiling the right sort of smile.

Catherine decided, for Lauren's sake, to let him down gently. "I'm terribly sorry." Meaning that she wasn't sorry, but would like to keep him as a client. "I will be busy that night, with a close friend." He didn't need to know that the close friend didn't exist. Let him assume that she had a lover. That would stave off any further invitations from him. She gave him a smile that she hoped looked properly sympathetic.

"Okay." He laughed, probably for Lauren's sake, showing that he wasn't upset. "It was worth a try."

"Thank you for the compliment." Catherine's smile took in both father and daughter. "Sure." He turned to Lauren. "Let's go, kid."

Catherine watched the taillights on Landry's truck flare, as he slowed at the gate before turning onto the road. Her shoulders slumped and she let weariness take control of her body. She had never felt more drained. There was no strength left in the muscles she had held rigid while she tried to appear alert and interested in her students. Landry's Valentine's Day party invitation had been the last straw that broke her. Her life seemed to be an endless succession of stumbling blocks that she tripped over instead of stepping across. It seemed that all of her efforts ended with some level of suffering. Today, her suffering included canceling a trip to the feed store that she no longer had the energy to even try.

She left her truck parked on the driveway and walked into the meadow where she stood with her arms wrapped around herself, gazing at the pine trees growing on the far side. A cold wind that threatened more winter rain whipped the branches to and fro, and bent the treetops. A pine cone fell silently onto the carpet of pine straw under the trees.

That's me, she thought, the victim of a storm with nothing to say about it.

Eight

*S*tudents from Stanford University crowded the café in downtown Palo Alto. When the weather turned fine, they came to town in droves, walking from the campus in groups of two, or three, or more, defying traffic on El Camino Real. The first day of April. April Fool's Day. A day for practical jokes. Whose sadistic idea was it, Catherine wondered, to set aside a special day for humiliating other human beings? After suffering as the target of Billy Raven's distorted sense of humor, she no longer saw anything funny about the tradition.

Making her way through the noisy crowd, she found a table beneath the wisteria covered trellis that shaded the brick terrace at one side of the café. The hum of bees among the purple blossoms joined the hum of happy voices. Rays of sunshine fell through the vines overhead onto the white linen tablecloth, and winked back from the silver flatware. In the middle of the table, a pair of pink cosmos tilted over

167

the rim of their vase on overlong stems that made the small flower arrangement seem precarious. Someone should cut them down to size, Catherine thought. The way someone should cut William Caldwell down to size. No, not William. Billy Raven. Or whoever! Catherine took a careful sip from her water glass, willing her hand not to shake.

Nearly two months had passed since she and Billy fought, and she still caught herself thinking that her handyman existed in some way distinct from her enemy, the famous Mr. Raven. She had no excuse for her continued confusion. Not after so many miserable weeks of mourning for one and hating the other.

Maude, her elderly landlady, had become a sympathetic ally. On the first day of March, when Catherine appeared at this same café, at the usual time, to share a pot of tea and turn over the rent check, Maude commented on her haggard appearance. "Dear girl, I can see that something terrible has happened. Tell me, what can I do to help you?"

Tears had filled Catherine's eyes. When she tried to speak, choking sobs shook her, making words impossible. The old woman wrapped her arms around Catherine, saying, "Hush, child, there's no need for you to say anything, just yet."

Maude signaled their waiter, and badgered Catherine into drinking quite a bit more sherry than she was used to. Her landlady asked no questions. Instead, Maude perched silently on her chair and kept Catherine company, taking hummingbird-size sips from her own glass of wine.

Later, while they ate the meal Maude ordered, Catherine related the whole sorry episode with Billy. "I loved him, how could he lie to me that way?" she cried.

"Dear, if women understood why men act like jackasses, we'd be jackasses ourselves."

"It takes one to know one, you mean." For a moment, a fleeting smile curved Catherine's lips. More wine with her meal had loosened her up enough to be able to smile just a little.

"Women are better at reading emotions. I heard somewhere that it's because we have more connections between the two halves of our brains than men do," Maude said.

"Oh, do men have brains?"

"Please, dear, I was just about to make a point."

"Okay. I'm listening." Catherine set her wine glass aside.

"I think your Billy may not have realized just how much pain he was causing you."

"He's not my Billy, not anymore," Catherine corrected.

"Be that as it may, dear, he probably thought you would forgive him, if not easily, at least eventually."

"Over my dead...no, over his dead body!" she exclaimed.

Maude laughed.

By the time they ended their meal with a rich chocolate mousse topped with fresh raspberries, and Maude had left in a taxi, Catherine was perfectly sober and, to her surprise, felt better. In fact, she felt well enough that night to sleep several hours straight for the first time since Billy broke her heart.

Now, one month later, Catherine looked forward to chatting with the older woman. Her friendship with Maude was the closest she had come to having the support of a loving mother. Maude's approval taught Catherine what she had been missing from her own mother, and, at the same time, helped Catherine see that she no longer needed what was impossible to get. She enjoyed every moment that she spent in Maude's reassuring company.

Catherine caught sight of Maude slowly walking toward her among the crowded tables on the patio. Maude wasn't alone. Sin was with her. Catherine's good spirits vanished at the sight of her brother. She hadn't spoken to him since the day she discovered his involvement in Billy's despicable game. She met her brother's anxious expression with a scowl.

"What's he doing here?" she demanded, before Maude had settled into her chair.

"Good afternoon, Catherine." Maude's pleasant greeting reprimanded Catherine for her outburst.

Catherine ducked her head. "Sorry, I'm not usually so rude."

"I know you're not, dear. We took you by surprise."

"Yes, you did." She shifted her attention onto her brother. "I'm not sure that I can sit at the same table with you."

Maude said, "Catherine, your brother is here at my urging. It is time to set things right."

Something about Maude's announcement made Catherine suspicious. She looked from the old woman to Sin, studying their somber faces. When her brother's eyes veered away and wouldn't meet her gaze, her suspicions grew. "What things?"

When Maude didn't answer immediately, Catherine focused on her brother for the answer. "Well, Sin, what else have you been lying to me about?"

Sin's troubled eyes turned to the old woman and she nodded encouragement. "Tell her," Maude said.

"Damn, this is hard." Sin took a shaky breath. "I convinced myself that I was helping you."

Catherine's anger surged so suddenly she nearly leaped out of her chair. "You thought ruining my life was helping me? How dare you!"

He shook his head. "I don't mean the thing with Billy. I mean before that."

"Before that? What are you talking about?" Catherine's head began to pound. She felt sick and was glad she hadn't eaten anything yet. It would be horrible to throw up in the midst of a public place.

"The farm." Sin's voice was abnormally soft, just above a whisper, as if speaking the two words out loud were condemning him to some personal hell.

"What about the farm? What's going on here?" She started to push her chair back from the table, ready to flee.

Maude reached over and put a restraining hand on Catherine's arm. "Please, hear him out. There have been enough secrets. It's time to begin repairing the damage."

Catherine felt desperate to avoid hearing whatever revelation came next. Sin and secrets were the most frightening combination that she could imagine. The next thing out of his mouth was bound to hurt her, and there was no way she could prepare, or protect herself.

Sin seemed equally desperate to keep her at the table. "Just listen, will you?"

Maude's hand tightened on her arm. There was steely determination in Maude's eyes.

Catherine couldn't jump up and tear herself from Maude's grip, without risking the old woman's fragile bones. Which, she knew, was exactly what Maude had planned. Catherine sighed and slumped back into her chair. She glared at her brother, "Say what you came here to say and get it over with."

"Go on, " Maude said to him.

Sin began, "When you first moved to the farm and were so insistent on being independent, well, I got worried."

"What's that got to do with anything?"

Sin gave her a weak smile. "Unfortunately, everything."

Catherine shook her head. "Explain, if you can," she said. "I can't despise you any more than I do already."

He winced at her choice of words, but stumbled on. "You put everything you had into the farm. All your energy and all your money."

"And all my dreams," Catherine added. She turned to Maude. "Are you about to tell me that I've lost the farm and just don't know it? I don't think I could bear that."

"No, that's not what we're telling you," Sin insisted. "But that is what I worried about. You're not rich like the rest of us. You invested your last dime in a venture I thought might turn out to be too great a risk."

"Oh, thank you for your vote of confidence." Catherine fumed at the thought of his distrust. "Have you forgotten that I've been around horses most of my life? Have you forgotten that I took care of our parents' business transactions for years? Do you think I'm an idiot?"

"I'm sorry for doubting you." Sin seemed earnest. "I see now that my worries were unjustified."

Catherine nodded. "I've made a good beginning, and I think my business will only get better." Catherine paused. So far, none of her earlier suspicions had been allayed. They'd gotten worse. Full of misgivings, she wondered, What sort of secret could involve both Sin and Maude?

Catherine studied her brother's face and found no hint of what he might say next. She forced herself to ask, "What has any of this to do with the farm?"

Sin said, "I convinced Maude to sell Hidden Lake Farm to me."

"Sell the farm to you? But I pay the rent to Maude every month." Catherine couldn't make sense of what he was saying. She frowned and watched him shift in his chair.

Sin's voice rose in pitch, as if a more desperate tone sounded more convincing. "That was part of our deal. So you wouldn't find out that I had backed you up, in case you got into financial trouble."

Catherine looked from Maude to her brother and back again. "You sold Hidden Lake Farm to Sin?"

Maude nodded. "He told me he loved you and I believed him. I still do."

"So, that's it? I owe my independence to my brother. I'm not sure what to say."

"You owe me nothing." The intensity of his denial surprised Catherine. "Your business has been doing very well. You haven't had any trouble paying the rent. My help wasn't needed."

"Your interference, you mean," Catherine corrected him.

"Yes, my interference. You're right, absolutely. I wish I'd kept out of it. I'm terribly sorry."

Catherine studied her brother's downcast expression. His regret seemed genuine. "Well," she said, "I guess you meant well." Catherine paused to consider the situation. "I don't think it makes much difference if you, or if Maude owns the farm. I'm still the tenant who holds the lease."

"That's right," Sin agreed. "It will be a business deal between the three of us. You'll still pay rent to Maude, since that is the way we set up the sale."

"Fine with me." Catherine smiled at the old woman. "I enjoy our monthly tea parties."

Maude patted her hand. "So do I, dear, so do I."

Sin said, "I don't expect you will forgive me so easily for siding with Billy, after I tell you what I've done."

Her brother's quiet comment alarmed Catherine. She gripped the edge of the table with both hands. Sin wouldn't look her in the eye. "What else have you done, Sin?"

Her brother's gaze remained fixed on the linen tablecloth. He hesitated, then blurted, "I leased the farmhouse to Billy's record company. They plan to film a music video there."

"Oh, no!" Catherine's eyes widened in horror. "How could you do that to me?"

"I saw how much you loved him. I imagined, foolishly I admit, that I could get the two of you back together."

Tractor-trailers clogged the driveway. Painted black, except for the silver Mercedes symbols gleaming on their prows, the huge vehicles were scattered about like a jumble of freight cars after a train wreck. None of the trucks bore identification. It seemed to Catherine that the CIA, or some other top secret government organization had gone into the moving business. She judged that two of the trailers housed dressing rooms. Retractable steps along their sides led up to each unmarked door. Curtained windows gave no hint of what might be going on inside the narrow rooms. All visible activity was taking place at the top of the driveway in front of the old house.

There, three of the massive vans were being unloaded onto the walkway just below the porch steps. Men scurried like aggravated ants, carrying mysterious objects in all directions. There seemed to be no coherent plan, as far as Catherine could see. It looked to her that things being carried into the house matched exactly the things being carried out of the house. Adding to the chaos, thick black electrical cables snaked across the bare ground in every direction.

As Catherine watched from a distance, she saw her brother tangle his foot in one of the cables and go down on one knee among the artificial shrubs set up next to the front steps by the invaders. Serves him right for inviting this madness, she thought, noting that Sin now walked with a slight limp, as he wandered off to observe the action elsewhere.

She might have been just as fascinated by the activities of the film crew as Sin seemed to be, if the army of strangers hadn't shattered the farm's peace and quiet, and frightened the horses. The rumble of diesel engines, the shouted commands and questions, and the banging of a dozen hammers had put an end to her curiosity.

She took the horses to the far side of the meadow to save them from the worst of the noise. Still, as she trudged back to the empty barn, she wondered where the members of Cherokee were hiding. She hadn't seen Billy Raven, or his huge friend, Carl, or anyone else who might be a rock legend pretending to be an ordinary person.

She rejected the idea that they occupied any of the mobile dressing rooms. The space behind those doors had to be very cramped. Rock stars lived in luxury. She couldn't imaging any of them stuffed into a dressing room the size of a gopher hole. She concluded that Billy Raven and his famous friends had yet to arrive.

Catherine turned her back on the commotion at the house and hurried into the barn. She glanced around the darkened interior and sighed. Ordinarily, a quiet calm filled the place—like the sense of peace that hikers experienced along green paths deep in a forest, or seekers found among the scattered stones of ancient temple ruins. Before, whenever she paused there during her morning chores, she felt at peace and content, as if an unseen presence eased her tension away. Now, standing beneath the roughhewn beams of the barn, she missed that feeling of security and comfort that had deserted her.

She hugged herself and wondered how she would survive the next few days. The knowledge that she and Billy would occupy the same small patch of land promised to turn every minute into a painful test of her courage. But she would not give him the satisfaction of seeing her suffer. She felt almost grateful to her mother, and her ability to devastate with offhand remarks disguised as pleasantries, which now served as a perfect example to imitate.

Catherine pictured her first meeting with Billy. She would stand before him aloof and slightly amused. She imagined his frustration when she refused to respond to him. She smiled at the thought, then felt ashamed that she had considered resorting to her mother's tactics, even for a few moments.

Off balance, and uncertain about what she should do, the screech of metal grating against metal startled her. Catherine whirled in the direction of the sound.

Someone had shoved the barn's massive door aside. Catherine squinted at the figure silhouetted against the sunlight and felt the floor lurch beneath her feet. Billy stepped through the open doorway into the barn.

Now that he stood before her, Catherine didn't want to confront him, she wanted to run from him. She clutched the door of the stall beside her and cried, "Get out!"

He took a step toward her. "Sweetheart, please, can't we talk?"

She turned her back on him. "There's nothing you can say that I want to hear, unless you've come to tell me that you and your oh-so-many friends are packing up and leaving."

"I'm sorry."

Delivered in the calm style she associated with his deliberately deceptive, totally invented character, William Caldwell, the two words covered the past, the present, and, she imagined, the immediate future. "Way too late, and way too little." She made no attempt to hide her bitterness.

Catherine heard him take another step toward her. She moved away down the corridor.

"Wait! he protested. "You wouldn't take my calls."

She spun around. "If you are trying to imply that any of this, this circus, is my fault..." She gestured wildly, flinging her arms toward the ruckus taking place on the driveway. "...then you are even more thickheaded than I thought."

"I hurt you."

"Yes, you did. But I'll get over it. And I'll get over you." She paused as a new thought struck her. "Actually, since the man I fell in love with doesn't exist, there's nothing to get over."

She turned and continued walking down the corridor. Catherine knew Billy intended to come after her, but just then someone called his name. She stopped and glanced back to the open barn door.

A man stood there. He embodied everything that Billy did not.

Where Billy seemed dark and dangerous, this man shone with light. His shoulder-length white hair caught the sun and shot it back in a ring of brightness around his gaunt face. Catherine remembered seeing paintings of medieval saints as she tagged along on tours of European art galleries with her father. No amount of gold leaf could equal the effect of this halo of light. It seemed as if the man's hair were some ethereal substance having a reality not of this earth, angel's hair bestowed upon a mere mortal.

When the stranger stepped into the shadowed interior of the barn, the glow of his shining hair dimmed, but did not die.

"Billy," the man's voice emerged as a ruined rasp, startling and unsettling, "the director wants you back at the house."

Billy swore, then turned toward Catherine. His obvious impatience tightened his lips and drew deep furrows across his brow. "This isn't finished. We'll talk later."

"I don't respond well to orders. You should know that by now, so don't give me any," she snapped.

Before he could respond, the other man said, "Billy, you're holding things up. They want your ideas on the first scene."

"Yeah, I hear you." Billy turned and stalked out of the barn.

It seemed to Catherine that he took all of the air with him. The effort it had taken for her to stand her ground, when she wanted to run away, left her drained and feeling dizzy. She slumped onto a bale of hay.

"You okay?" The raspy voice spoke close to her ear.

Catherine raised her chin and blinked, clearing unshed tears from her eyes. "I'm fine." The medieval angel stooped over her, his human features softened by concern. "You don't look fine. Your face is sort of pale."

Gentleness seemed at odds with the strange quality of his voice. She blurted out her thoughts. "How do you sing?"

The man laughed. The rich sound carried all the melody that the jarring quality of his speaking voice lacked. "Very badly!"

His smile, when he turned it on her, conveyed nothing saintly. He looked her up and down in an insolent, assessing way. "So, you're Billy's woman."

Catherine scrambled to her feet. "I'm nobody's woman, but my own!"

His smile widened.

No, not saintly at all, Catherine decided. She frowned back at him.

Undeterred, he asked, "Want to show me around your barn?"

"Not particularly. I'm not in the mood to play any more games with the filthy rich and influential."

If anything, his smile grew more intense, and full of devilment.

"Not even if it makes Billy mad as hell?"

She asked, "What makes you think I might want to do that?"

"Let's just say that I admired the architecture of the barn for quite some time, before I announced my presence."

"You mean you were eavesdropping." She didn't know whether to be angry at the invasion of her privacy, or grateful for his well-timed intrusion into what had threatened to become a rather nasty scene between herself and Billy Raven.

"Admiring the eaves. Eavesdropping. I get them confused sometimes." He laughed again, but this time his laugh seemed slightly sinister.

A prickle of unease ran down Catherine's spine. Dark looks gave Billy a dangerous image, but this man truly might be dangerous. And he seemed to have a grudge against Billy.

"Why would you want to hurt him?" she demanded.

"Not hurt." He shook his head, rejecting her notion. "If I wanted him hurt, I'd just drag Billy behind this barn and beat the crap out of him."

Catherine had no doubt that he could and would do just that. The man projected an intensity unlike any she had ever known, a constant tension that spoke of violence held in check by rigid self-discipline. She wanted to ask him what dark event had damaged him, but feared what she might discover.

"If you don't intend to hurt him, what do you intend?"

"To annoy the hell out of him for as long as I can, before he tries to beat the crap out of me." He grinned, and Catherine realized he delighted in conflict in the same way a dedicated gourmet delights in a sumptuous meal, as something to be savored. The idea chilled her. And, oddly, it reassured her at the same time. She knew he wouldn't take the quarrel too far. That would spoil his fun.

"You haven't explained why." Before she decided to form what had to be an unholy alliance with the man, she wanted to know what sort of dispute she might be joining.

"Billy's been acting a little highhanded lately. It's been pissing me off."

"That's it? That's all it takes to turn you against a friend? That's preposterous." She couldn't believe that two grown men would spar with each other instead of talking things over. Or that one of them thought quarreling was fun.

"I like my freedom. A lot. Billy's been getting in my way," he responded, defiant.

Catherine said, "Look, I don't think I want to get involved in a war, even a limited one. So thanks, but no thanks. I'll deal with Billy on my own, in my own way." She took a step back.

"You're sure?" He peered at her, his face altered by an expression that made her want to back up some more. "Revenge can be very sweet," he told her.

"I'm sure it can, but it's not really my style. I'm not ready to go that far, and I'm not so sure I'd feel better afterward if I did." That she had even thought about it, unsettled her.

"Suit yourself." He strolled away.

"Wait!" she called after him. "Which one are you?"

"John," he said over his shoulder, "lead guitar."

At midday, Catherine packed a carton of strawberry yogurt, a few carrot sticks, and two chocolate chip cookies into a plastic bag, and grabbed a small bottle of sparkling cider. She wore a broad-brimmed hat to shield her face from the sun. Outside, she turned her back on the film crew and headed toward the lake. She was so preoccupied with the problem of how to avoid Billy until she could put into action a strategy for dealing with him, she didn't notice that the chaos on the opposite side of the driveway had wound down. The film crew had gathered at long tables arranged beneath a blue and white canopy next to the catering truck. Conversation had replaced the sound of hammers.

Catherine smiled as she strolled across the meadow. Her little herd of horses stood in the shade of the pines bordering the lake. The horses were busy with the lush spring grass and paid little attention to her as she made her way among them and through the trees. She reached the narrow path that hugged the edge of the lake and paused, as she always did, to look at the view.

The surface of the water, still as a sheet of glass on this windless day, reflected the encircling trees and the azure sky above so faithfully, the earth and sky seemed to have traded places. Catherine found it strange that no ducks floated on the water. No birds sang from the branches of the pines. Unnatural silence brooded all around. Catherine stared across the lake toward the grassy spot tucked among the rocks.

A woman's shriek broke the silence, followed by masculine laughter and the sounds of splashing. A jay rose like a swift blue dart from the grove of madrone trees, scolding its outrage. Equally outraged that Billy had taken another woman to her private retreat, Catherine rushed along the path to confront him and his female companion.

The sight that greeted her left her more breathless than her dash around the lake. Four couples occupied the sun drenched grass. All of them were naked. Their tangled limbs made identification difficult, but none of the men had long, dark hair. The fact that Billy was not among the trespassers freed her from most of her anger. She surveyed the group with appalled curiosity.

She had met one of the trespassers already. John stood in water up to his waist, embraced by a soaking wet Hollywood starlet. Catherine's eyes popped wide. The woman had appeared, fully clothed, in a recent television commercial for a major internet provider. At present, her arms and legs were plastered to John like starfish tentacles stuck to a doomed fish, while she fed on his body. Her open mouth sucked the water from his pale skin, leaving distinct marks. He didn't seem to mind the small pain she caused. Catherine felt sick.

She must have made some sound, because John turned toward her. Their eyes met. His eyes lighted with amusement. He dropped the woman with a splash and ignored her as she came to the surface of the water, sputtering and indignant. He strode toward Catherine through the waves caused by the starlet's fall. Lake water poured from his hard-muscled physique as he gained the shore. The patterns on the rest of his body attested to the fact that his extraordinary white hair had not been dyed. She tried to keep her eyes centered on his face.

"Darling," he observed, "you've got too many clothes on." He reached out and tipped the hat from her head.

She took two steps back, making space between them. "Keep your hands to yourself."

He gestured toward the starlet, now dripping onto the grass and glaring at them. "Some ask just the opposite."

"Not me"

"Ah," he nodded, "not enough privacy. I'll get rid of the others."

"No."

"Afraid?" He stepped close.

This time Catherine held her ground. "Any woman not afraid of you is out of her mind."

He laughed. Great gasps of amusement shook his shoulders. He caressed her cheek with his fingertips. "I see why Billy is so besotted with you. You tell everything like it is. How refreshing."

"If you find the truth refreshing, your life stinks."

Her statement increased his approval of her. He repeated it to the bunch of avid spectators seated on the grass. The others joined in the laughter.

Just what I need, Catherine thought, the unfettered praise of a psychopath.

"If I put on my pants, will you have lunch with me?"

She held out the plastic bag she carried. "Brought my own."

He inspected the contents. "Crap."

When he tried to pull the bag out of her hand and toss it into the lake, she batted his hand away. "I told you, hands off!"

"We're having barbecued spareribs, poached salmon, half a dozen different salads and chocolate mousse. Catered. The best cuisine money can buy."

"Not impressed. You'll have to up the ante."

"Champagne?" he inquired.

"Not before six o'clock in the evening." She attempted to look prim.

186

John cocked his head to one side, pretending to be coy, and grinned at her. "My guarantee that Billy will be irritated out of his gourd?"

"I thought we agreed to disagree about that this morning," Catherine said.

"It was worth a second try."

"Too bad."

"What would it take to convince you?"

John's lunch invitation gave her a chance to see Billy again, on her terms, and in front of witnesses. Catherine wanted to give him a piece of her mind, and she didn't trust herself to do it in private. She replied, "Mention chocolate mousse one more time, and put all your clothes on."

She turned her back on the frolicking nudists and set off for her apartment. She intended to put the carton of yogurt back in her refrigerator before she joined John at the catering truck. But her lunch date caught up with her at the edge of the woods.

"Chocolate mousse!" John said the words in the same way that children cry, "Open Sesame," and spun in a circle to show her his clothing.

He wore designer jeans and deerskin moccasins. The jeans were black and the moccasins looked authentic. His sleeveless black t-shirt showed off some of the tattoos she had refused to notice while he stood naked two feet in front of her.

Now, she inspected both arms. Realistic barbed wire wrapped itself around his biceps. Celtic runes circled one wrist. The lovely face of a woman with intricately braided, flaxen tresses adorned with emeralds and opals peered back at her from his right shoulder.

"Leave any ink in the inkwell?" she inquired.

"You're a sassy piece, aren't you?"

"Not usually. There's something about you that brings out the worst in me."

"Thanks." He looked pleased.

"That wasn't meant as a compliment."

"Anyone can be polite," he said. "It takes talent and practice, and keen observation of other people's faults to become truly annoying."

Like my brother, she thought. "John, you're a fraud," she accused.

He shrugged. "Maybe so, maybe not."

They stepped through the door into her apartment. While she emptied the contents of the plastic bag into the refrigerator, he strolled farther into the room.
"This is nice," he said. "Primitive, but cozy. Too bad you don't have a fireplace."

"Why?" She had to ask, even though she suspected his praise of her home, coupled with the one short-coming, was the start of more of the verbal jousting that he enjoyed.

True to form, he smiled at her and said, "Firelight reflected in your beautiful eyes would make you even more alluring, while we made love on one of those homemade braided rugs."

Catherine let out a whoop of laughter. "You're outrageous!"

"Yes, I believe I am." He threw a tattooed arm about her shoulders and steered her out of the apartment door and over to the catering truck.

Billy sat with several people at one of the long tables. The look he shot her held no hint of invitation and let Catherine know he objected to her choice of escort. John proved to be just as keen an observer of others as he had claimed, and tightened his arm around her. Billy's remote expression became even more forbidding.

Catherine's smiling companion pulled out a chair across from his target. "Shall we sit here?" John asked her, overly polite, overly bright, for Billy's benefit.

Smarting from the cold reception she received, Catherine said, "Sure, why not?"

"Why not, indeed?" John winked at her. "What would you like to eat? Salad? Salmon? Ribs?"

"How about a salad sampler? A bit of each kind, if that's okay?"

"Coming right up!" He moved off to the open counter at the back of the caterer's truck.

"Don't forget the mousse," she called after him.

Billy stared at her in stony silence. Defiant, Catherine stared back. Conversation at the table came to a standstill. Crew members seated at either end of the table watched them with rapt expressions. Someone whistled under his breath, as tension built over the cobalt blue china and sparkling sterling silver flatware. No one moved.

"What game are you playing?" Billy asked at last.

"You're the master game player, you tell me," she countered.

"John isn't a chess piece you can push around at will," he warned.

"Neither am I," Catherine said.

"I never thought you were."

"Oh, please! Everything you do shows how little respect you have for me." She gestured toward the others sitting at the same table. "You brought these people here, when you knew I would hate it."

"Sin told me that you had agreed."

"Never!" she cried.

"By the time I found out the truth, all the contracts had been signed. "

"Contracts have been broken before. You could have gone somewhere else."

"Not without putting a lot of people out of work. Some of the crew turned down other jobs to work on this one."

A couple of the men seated at the table nodded in agreement. Catherine glared at them. She said, "You're rich. You could have paid them anyway."

Billy shook his head. "You don't know much about entertainment industry unions. Nobody's that rich."

"So my needs come last."

Before he could reply, the laughing voices of two small children stopped him. Redheaded twins rushed up to the table, followed by a man who looked like an older, taller version of the little boys. His companion, an attractive woman dressed in sandals, jeans, and a pink t-shirt with what looked like orange juice spilled down the front, had to be their mother. The two kids elbowed each other as they both climbed onto Billy's lap.

"Uncle Billy, Uncle Billy, here we are!"

The adults at the table turned smiling faces upon the children. Hostilities had ended for the time being.

"Well, if it isn't Pete and Repeat!" Billy exclaimed.

"Are you Pete?" one brother inquired of the other. Both boys giggled.

The second twin said, "Repeat!"

"Are you Pete?" the first twin asked louder.

"Repeat!" the other shouted. Giggles became belly laughs.

Catherine watched the twins with a grin. No one could resist the antics of the carrot-topped pair. She looked up at the red-haired man and his wife, saw the pride in their eyes, and felt a moment's envy. How lucky the boys were to have such doting parents.

She felt Billy's eyes on her, and turned to meet his gaze. She saw sympathy there and felt herself flush. She hadn't realized that Billy knew her so well. She looked away.

"Catherine," Billy said, "this is George and this is Henry." Billy pointed first to one boy and then to the other. "Or this is Henry and this is George."

He sounded puzzled and peered at them as if terribly nearsighted. Both boys burst into gales of laughter, nearly falling off Billy's lap.

Their father introduced himself and his wife. "I'm Rick, and this lovely creature wearing the orange juice is Molly."

A couple of crew members gave their seats to the newcomers. John returned a moment later and placed a plate heaped with colorful salads in front of Catherine. He made a production of offering her a small bowl of chocolate mousse, bowing and simpering and playing the part of an groveling waiter. "As madam requested," he said, then ended his performance by turning toward Billy to gauge his reaction. Satisfied, John took the empty chair next to hers.

"Where's Carl?" John asked.

"He'll be here around five this evening," Rick said. "Filming isn't due to start until it gets dark. Anyway, Carl's in no hurry."

"Carl's chicken," John told Catherine. "He's afraid of you."

"What?" She darted a glance at Billy.

He nodded, and said, "He thinks you might be holding a grudge."

"But it wasn't his fault. He didn't lie to me."

John slid his arm around her shoulders once again. "Yeah, Billy, who do you suppose the liar might be?"

Catherine resented John's newest attempt to enlist her in his on-going feud with Billy. Sitting tucked against his side made her look like John's ally, but before she could slide from under his arm, matters were taken out of her hands.

Rick cleared his throat. "No games in front of the kids, man," he reminded John.

"What game?" George piped up, lifting a curious face toward his father.

"What game?" echoed Henry.

John looked contrite. "Sorry."

Billy handed George and Henry off to their father and rose to his feet. "I've had enough." No one thought that he was talking about salmon and ribs. To Catherine, he added in a cool tone, "Enjoy your lunch."

She watched him stride, stiff-backed and angry, toward the old house. Several crew members already walked in that direction. Billy caught up with them, and without a backward glance, climbed the steps to the front porch and disappeared inside the open door.

Beside her, John took his arm from around her and stretched like a canary-filled cat. His face wore a satisfied smile. "That was fun," he commented.

Catherine twisted in her chair to glare at him. "I didn't ask you to butt in. I told you before that I'd deal with Billy in my own way."

Molly reached across the table and touched Catherine's hand. "Don't mind John, he just can't resist stirring up trouble. We're all used to it."

"He can create as much chaos as he wants in someone else's life, but not in mine," Catherine declared.

"Can we drop the subject?" Rick tilted his head down toward the boys perched on his lap. Their heads swiveled from Catherine to John to their mother, waiting for the next addition to the fascinating discussion.

Catherine pushed her chair back from the table. "I'm not very hungry."

"Oh, don't go," Molly said. "I was looking forward to getting to know you."

John hummed a few bars of music from *The King and I,* his sarcasm aimed at Molly. She smiled at him and said, "Shut up."

Catherine got to her feet. "I'm sorry, Molly, I'm not in a very sociable mood right now. So, if you will excuse me..."

John reached for the chocolate mousse. "No dessert? I guess I'll have to eat it myself."

Wishing she could hurry back to the barn, but forcing herself to stroll casually, Catherine said, "Be my guest."

John called after her, "It's such a relief to know that I'm no longer trespassing!"

Nine

Two unexpected things happened during the afternoon. Catherine was keenly aware of both.

A line of bright yellow tape, strung between wooden stakes driven into the ground along the length of the driveway, appeared on the side closest to the barn. The tape was printed in black ink every few feet with the words 'No Admittance.' Catherine assumed the tape was an attempt to provide her with some belated privacy.

Promising the opposite, two luxurious motor homes arrived and parked fender to fender in a level area just inside the farm's iron gate. Catherine watched Molly and the twins enter the one nearest the road. The other, she surmised with a sinking feeling, must belong to Billy Raven. She knew he was in charge of Cherokee's business activities, she should have realized that he would stay on the farm to supervise the film crew's work. That meant she couldn't avoid chance meetings with Billy during the eight days the movie crew was scheduled to remain at the farm, thanks to her brother. There was nothing she could do about it. She decided to keep her back turned toward the two motor homes for the rest of the afternoon. And maybe, if she felt like it, for seven more days.

At dusk, the sounds coming from the direction of the catering truck told her that the movie crew had gathered for another sumptuous meal. Cheerful conversation and laughter drifted across the driveway, over the yellow tape, and into the barn. With renewed energy, Catherine scrubbed saddle soap into the leather bridle draped across her knees. During the long afternoon she had found several chores to keep her busy and out of sight. Two saddles, gleaming like new, rested on a nearby bale of hay. More bridles lay at her feet, awaiting their portion from the can of saddle soap that sat on the floor beside them.

Catherine thought about the lunch she turned down and imagined the gourmet delights the movie crew was enjoying at that moment. Suddenly, she was starving. She frowned at the bridle in her hands. While she hid in the barn, everyone else had gone about their business without regard to emotional outbursts, or grudges.

"Stupid, stupid, stupid," she scolded herself. Denying herself the pleasure of eating lunch with Molly and the children had no effect on Billy. She was the one who had missed out. Catherine felt angry with herself for running from Billy's friends, simply because she assumed that they would take his side against her. She had overreacted to seeing him again, and her behavior seemed childish and self-defeating. Her decision to avoid Billy robbed her of the chance to show him how little he mattered to her now.

The movie crew's invasion of Hidden Lake Farm was more Sin's fault than Billy's. From that standpoint, both she and Billy were victims of her brother's meddling. She had managed to forgive Sin for interfering in her life, because he had done it out of misguided brotherly love.

Maybe I ought to be more understanding of Billy's situation, as least as far as the filming of Cherokee's music video goes, she reasoned. She could accept his presence on the farm for a few days. And do it with good grace. She was that strong. But his deception of her was quite separate and, measured on a scale of heartache, absolutely unforgivable.

Catherine wiped the excess saddle soap off the bridle she'd been cleaning and dropped it on the floor with the others. The task could wait for another day. She marched into her apartment and began preparing her supper. It wasn't exactly gourmet, just a baked potato topped with spicy canned chili and a pile of grated sharp cheese.

Darkness fell while she ate. She remembered someone saying that the movie crew was supposed to start filming as soon as the sky turned dark, so activity at the old house would be reaching its peak. She wondered what Billy would think, if she took a look. No doubt he would greet her with the same lack of welcome she got from him at lunch. So what? she thought. *If I want to watch a bunch of Hollywood actors film a video, then that's what I'm going to do.* She refused to be treated as an outsider in her own home. She grabbed a jacket and headed out the apartment's back door.

On her back porch, she collided headfirst with Sin's chest. "Ow! What are you doing here?" she said, rubbing her squashed nose.

Her brother peered at her from beneath arched brows. "I came to see if you were still being stubborn."

" At the moment I am being slightly wounded."

"Wounded, but still able to walk," he said. "Come watch the movie makers. It's fun."

"I was on my way there, when you bashed into me."

"The way I remember it, you bashed into me. But who cares? I had in mind dragging you across the driveway into enemy territory." Sin grinned at her.

"If you try to drag me anywhere, I might have in mind a couple of black eyes..." She gazed into his eyes. "...instead of those pretty green ones."

He laughed and tucked his sister's arm through his. "Wait until you see all the actors in their makeup. Spooky as hell."

"I imagine so." She couldn't muster as much excitement as her brother, not while she expected another awkward meeting with Billy. Her steps slowed.

"Come on," Sin urged. "I don't want to miss anything interesting."

A crowd had gathered in front of the house. Lights supported on four steel towers arranged in a semicircle on the mostly dead lawn were trained on the shallow steps that led to the porch. Two cameras focused on the scene from different angles. Crew members milled about, engaged in activities that seemed disorganized to Catherine's untrained eyes. Among the bystanders, she recognized Carl's huge form towering over Molly and Rick. The twins were nowhere in sight. Catherine followed her brother through the crowd toward the action taking place on the porch steps. When Carl moved over, making room for her at the front of the group, she understood the children's absence.

Spotlighted on the steps, John's friend from the lake now clung to Billy, her thin figure plastered to his naked chest. He stood immobile as she crawled her way up his body. Her scarlet lips opened wide and covered his mouth. She draped one fragile arm around Billy's neck, and her other hand slid lower and lower, not stopping at his belt buckle. If anything, the starlet seemed to be wearing less this evening than she had at noon. Wispy scarves, thin as cobwebs, hid little as they swayed languidly in breezes coming from fans placed just out of camera range. Catherine stared at the two and told herself that the emotion raging through her had nothing to do with jealousy.

"Hold it, hold it!" The director stepped onto the porch and dropped a hand on the starlet's shoulder. "Look, sweetheart, you're a demon. When you kiss him, make it sexy, make it evil."

The girl nodded and tossed her head back, exposing her long white throat, ready to lunge forward and fasten her mouth over Billy's.

"That looks good." The director turned toward the extras crowding the porch, all of them wore pale gray body paint and tattered rags. He gestured at the ghouls and waved his arms to indicate they should bunch even closer together. "Places, everyone," he said.

John pushed through the bystanders and slid into a narrow space beside Catherine. He asked, "Would you believe I was helping her rehearse her part while we were at the lake?"

"Not for one split second," she told him.

The director yelled, "Action!"

The sex-crazed demon-girl tried to suck Billy's brains out through his mouth. Catherine felt heat rising in her cheeks and focused her eyes on the toes of her boots. John slung an arm around her waist and pulled her close. "Hot stuff, huh? She's good."

Carl said, "I'm gonna need a cold shower."

"Or a warm woman," John replied, holding Catherine tighter. He whispered in her ear, "You can look, now. They're done with the disgusting part."

She raised her head. The ghouls carried the girl off into the house. Billy remained slumped in a heap on the steps. The director shouted, "Cut! Fantastic! Thanks everybody."

Dismissed, the actors scattered, some headed for their dressing rooms, some toward the caterer's truck where snacks had been laid out on one of the tables. Sin elbowed his way out of the audience of bystanders and followed close on the heels of a shapely, gray-painted girl who was headed for the food. Catherine smiled at the sight of ghouls helping themselves to slices of pizza, and stuffing freshly baked sour dough rolls with cold cuts. Rick and Molly strolled off, arms linked, heads close together, in the direction of their motor home. Rick said something and Molly giggled. Catherine looked for Billy and discovered him sitting on the porch steps. His angry eyes drilled into hers. Distracted by the moviemaking, she had forgotten that John's arm still circled her waist. Carl murmured, "Billy's real pissed."

Alarm filled her as Billy rose to his feet. Catherine tried to step away from John, but his grip on her tightened and he held her fast. She felt John shrug as he drawled, "I'm so afraid."

Carl took several steps back, out of range of any sudden physical expressions of displeasure. "Man, this time you're really pushing it."

"Do you think so?" John asked. Catherine noted that his eyes never left Billy. Nor did Billy's gaze shift from her.

With both hands, she pushed against John's arm. It wouldn't budge.

"Let her go." Billy's unemotional tone cut like a knife, and Catherine felt grateful that he was speaking to John and not to her.

"Please, John," she said. Fear made her voice tremble.

John glanced down at her. "For you, anything." His lips brushed over her temple. Billy grasped her upper arm and pulled her toward him. "We're not done with this," he warned John.

"It will be my pleasure to accommodate you any time you like. Swords or pistols?" John gave a slight bow, and straightened wearing a charming smile.

"Shove it!" Billy replied.

Instead of releasing Catherine, Billy forced her at high speed in the direction of his private trailer. He dragged her stumbling up the steps and through the door. The door slammed shut. He towered over her, half naked and covered with another woman's scarlet lipstick. "Listen, you silly little girl, I warned you about John. What the hell do you think you're doing?"

Catherine shouted, "Don't you dare call me names!"

He stepped forward and she backed up until she collided with the sofa. She sat down so hard she bounced, but still managed to fix him with a furious gaze.

He said, "I'll call you whatever I damn well please! You're in a whole lot of trouble and you don't even know it."

"So, I'm silly," she agreed. "Is that it? Can I go now?" She mimicked the dull tone of a defiant teenager. Her attitude inflamed Billy.

"Shut up and listen!" he ordered. "If you want to fool around with someone like John, you ought to know something about your new playmate."

"I prefer to make up my own mind about people. I do not listen to gossip." She glared at him, but didn't move from the sofa. In his current mood, if she got up, Billy might toss her back down again.

He said, "Truth doesn't qualify as gossip."

She shook her head. "Not interested."

"Oh, for God's sake, for once in your life, let somebody take care of you for a change."

"How?" she asked. "By letting him manhandle me and yell at me?"

Billy swore. "Damn it. John is difficult as hell. He's unpredictable. He could hurt you."

"Thanks for the warning. As I said, I pick my own friends." Thinking they had both said enough, she started to rise from the sofa.

"You will sit there while I tell you a story," he commanded.

His stony expression convinced Catherine to remain seated. She leaned back against the cushions. "Since you insist," she said, "I have no choice but to listen."

"Fine, so listen."

She shrugged and he began.

"Once upon a time there was a little boy, a toddler. We don't know exactly how old he was because there are no records of his birth. We don't know his name, so let's call him John Doe. One day, little Johnny's mother overdosed on meth and died. Little Johnny found her on the floor of their rented room. His mother looked awful and Johnny was frightened. He began to scream and woke his mother's boyfriend, a drug dealer. The boyfriend tried to quiet Johnny, first by beating him and then by strangling him. The man who lived in the next room heard shouting and kicked in the door. If he hadn't stopped the drug dealer, little Johnny would be dead. Instead, Johnny spent a long time in the hospital recovering from broken bones. His voice was just as broken, and still is. For some reason, his hair turned white. His hostility to adults made him unlovable. He grew up in a series of foster homes. Now, he plays lead guitar for Cherokee. We cut him a lot of slack, but we aren't stupid enough to think we can play his mind games without getting roughed up in the process."

While Billy watched her in silence, Catherine sat on the sofa deep in thought. The blunt recounting of John's sordid history shocked her, as Billy intended. Yet, as her shock eased, something beyond her irritation with John took its place. John had suffered more than she could imagine. Still, he had made a success of his life, against terrible odds. Admiration for him pushed aside the last of her misgivings about him.

Catherine gazed up into Billy's angry face and said, "John has done nothing to hurt me. Less, in fact, than you have done. I see no reason to reject his friendship."

The next morning, Catherine awoke much earlier than usual. Her rumpled bed was a witness to her restless night. So was the face looking back at her from her mirror. The makeup she hadn't touched in over a year, but still kept in a kitchen drawer, suddenly became useful. The dark circles under her eyes disappeared under a coat of concealer and a dusting of loose powder.

A second dusting of blush corrected the lack of color in her cheeks. Pink gloss gave a slight sheen to dry, bitten lips. A cup of coffee and a walk beside the lake would take care of the rest.

The sun was a faint glimmer on the horizon when she left her apartment and headed across the meadow. Her passing footsteps cut a dew-drenched path through the tall grass, soaking the cuffs of her jeans. She didn't mind. The clean, clear air that had brought the dew during the night swept her head of emotional cobwebs. She and Billy didn't have to agree about John. She and Billy didn't have to agree about anything. She and Billy were not a couple. They'd had a very brief affair, if a few passionate kisses could be called an affair, but now it was over. There was nothing more to discuss. There wouldn't be any repeats of last night's confrontation. If she wasn't exactly indifferent to Billy, she wasn't pining for him anymore, either. Catherine picked up her pace, wanting to watch the sun rise over Hidden Lake.

On her way back from the lake, Catherine discovered that she had company waiting for her near the barn.

"Miss O'Shea, Miss O'Shea!" George and Henry hung as far as they could over the yellow tape barrier beside the driveway. "Can we see the horses? Puleeeeese?"

Catherine strolled in their direction. "Hi, guys. You're up and out very early." She glanced at her watch. No one else from among the overnight visitors seemed to be stirring.

Henry said, "The sun is up."

Catherine nodded. "Yes, it is."

George explained, "Mommy says we can't leave our room until the sun comes up."

"Smart Mommy." Catherine smiled at the boys.

"Can we see the horses?" Henry asked again.

"Oh," she said to him, "you must be Repeat." She turned to George. "And you must be Pete."

"That's just a funny game," he said, shaking his head. "I'm George." He turned around to display the back of his t-shirt. "See?"

A caricature of George Washington boldly standing in a rowboat, crossing an icy river, filled the back of George's shirt. She recognized her brother's handiwork. "Let me see yours," she said to Henry.

Henry spun around. King Henry VIII frowned at her from beneath a golden crown. The king stood in the center of a circle of his unsmiling wives. One wife held a red-haired baby in her arms. The baby's mouth was wide open in an angry howl, her brother's vision of the future Queen of England, Elizabeth I.

Catherine laughed. She felt certain that neither boy appreciated the history lessons splashed in cartoon colors on the backs of their shirts.

"My brother has been busy." She grinned at the boys and their heads bobbed up and down in agreement.

"He's fun," said Henry.

"Yeah," said George. "He let us paint a shirt for him. It's got handprints and squiggles and spots and stuff."

"It sounds fantastic. I can't wait to see him wearing it."

"We put lots of paint on. It isn't dry yet." George sounded uncertain about the outcome of their efforts.

"Maybe he'll wear it tomorrow," Henry suggested.

"Maybe so," she agreed.

"Can we come over?" Henry asked. Catherine noticed that sometimes one twin took the lead in their adventures, sometimes the other. Both seemed very bright.

Catherine told them, "Not without your mother's permission."

"Okay! Okay!" they yelled. "We'll be right back."

Catherine smiled as George and Henry bounded down the driveway toward their motor home.

A few minutes later the boys returned, followed by Molly, looking somewhat disheveled. She held a large blue china mug in one hand. With the other hand, she swept her uncombed hair off of her face. Her eyes, still puffy from sleep, focused a long-suffering gaze on Catherine.

"I could have used about eight more hours of sleep," she said. "Thank God, Billy was up and had brewed some coffee." She took a sip from the mug and sighed. "The best money can buy."

"Of course," Catherine said. She had served him an inexpensive supermarket brand. "Only the best for Billy." Her bitter tone drew a sharp glance from Molly.

To head off any further mention of Billy, Catherine lifted the yellow tape high enough for the boys to scoot underneath, and said, "Shall we go take a look at the horses?"

Joyous shouts greeted her invitation. The twins dashed toward the barn. She and Molly sped after them. As the boys disappeared through the open barn door, Catherine called, "Wait for us!"

Obedient, the twins skidded to a stop just inside the stable entrance, where they hopped up and down in excitement, and shouted, "Hurry, hurry!"

Molly sighed dramatically and rolled her eyes. "It's like this all day long. They take everything at full speed and at the top of their lungs."

"Poor you," Catherine replied with a grin.

"No, poor you." Molly laughed. "Let's see if you can keep them from dismantling your barn."

Catherine took each boy by the hand and guided them down the central corridor of the building. The horses, expecting to be fed, poked their heads out of their stalls.

"Look, look!" George shouted to his brother, pointing at Admiral. "The black stallion!" The horse snorted at the noisy child and retreated into the depths of his stall.

"A black stallion," Catherine corrected. "And not like the one in the movie. This one is much too dangerous for you to ride."

With their fantasies momentarily overruled, the boys towed her toward the next stall where the big dapple gray watched them with twitching ears. Catherine said, "He likes carrots. Do you want to feed him?" She pulled a chunk of carrot out of her pocket and held it out to the horse on the palm of her hand. "Like this," she said, "with your hand held flat so he doesn't bite your fingers by mistake."

Squirming with delight, the boys fed carrots to the horse. "Can we ride him?" Henry asked.

Catherine darted a glance at their mother, who nodded her approval. "This horse is a bit headstrong for beginning riders, but I have another horse that you can ride, if you're both very quiet and do just what I tell you to do."

When she led the sorrel mare out of her stall, Henry whispered to his mother with enough volume for the whole barn to hear, "Mommy, is that the red horse she let Uncle Billy ride?"

Catherine turned toward Molly in shocked disbelief. Everyone, even the twins, knew of her disastrous few days with Billy.

Molly's expression was full of understanding and sympathy. She said, "After Billy left here, he came to us. He was pretty cut up about what happened."

"So cut up that he discussed my private affairs in front of the children?" She tugged on the lead rope and walked the mare out of the barn toward the arena. The two boys darted ahead.

Molly hurried after Catherine. "They knew nothing about you and Billy until a few days ago, when we told them we would be staying on your farm to make a music video."

"Well, I wouldn't be surprised to see him on some television talk show blabbing how he'd been run off the road by a country bumpkin horse trainer too stupid to recognize him. He'd get a big laugh out of that story."

Molly shook her head. "That's not possible."

"Why not? Think of the publicity he'd get."

"Billy doesn't want, or need, that kind of publicity. He'd never splash his personal life on television, or in the tabloids."

"But he'd splash my personal life on a movie set. Everyone seems to know what happened between us."

"Just the band and me," Molly assured her. "Nobody else."

"That's a few too many, in my opinion."

"When Billy went missing, we found him here. What was he supposed to say?"

Catherine shrugged. "How about nothing?"

Molly persisted. "When Carl barged in and triggered a huge blow up? Some explanation had to be made."

"Oh, I can hear it now. Ha, ha. What a joke. She didn't recognize me, and I lived there for three whole days."

Catherine brought the mare to a stop in the center of the arena beside the two boys. The twins stood quietly, both wearing huge grins.

"That's nonsense," Molly insisted, her voice pitched too low for the twins to hear.

Catherine ignored her and stooped to lift Henry onto the mare's back. "Henry, sit up straight and hold tight to her mane with both hands. It won't hurt her and it will help you balance."

She turned to George and said, "Stay right where you are and watch carefully. When it's your turn, you will already know what to do." To Molly she added,

"Will you walk on the other side of the mare, just in case?"

"Just in case what?" Henry asked.

"Just in case you fall off like your Uncle Billy did." Henry nodded, all seriousness. Molly laughed. "Billy left out that part of the story."

By the time both boys had taken a turn, bouncing like redheaded ping pong balls on the back of the good natured mare, Catherine had fallen in love. For the first time in her life, she thought about having a child of her own. Her mother had been such a dismal example of motherhood, Catherine never pictured herself in that role. Now, she considered the possibility that someday she might guide her own child around the arena on the back of a gentle, sweet-tempered pony. She imagined a little boy, not quite as old as the twins. He would have her blue eyes and his father's raven hair. A lovely child.

Catherine swore under her breath. Billy's child. Some emotion had overpowered her common sense and had taken her by surprise. For those few short hours, before her dreams had been shattered, when she had allowed herself to love Billy, she hadn't once thought of bearing his children. At least not consciously. Apparently, some secret part of her heart had clung to other hopes. The discovery was doubly painful, because those hopes would never be fulfilled. The wildly handsome, cheerfully casual car thief had vanished from her life, and in his place, Billy Raven loomed, more a threat than a promise of lasting happiness. Nothing her heart pictured included a life of glitter and public acclaim. For a moment, Catherine felt ill and leaned against the side of the mare for support.

She heard Molly say, "Ride's over. Now, breakfast." Both boys began to plead for another turn, but their mother stood firm. "Catherine has been very kind to let you take up so much of her time. Now, scoot." She pointed toward the trailers. "Uncle Billy said he would make breakfast for you." The boys took off at a run.

Catherine turned away and led the mare toward the barn. Breakfast with Uncle Billy seemed to be part of a larger plan to leave Molly free to spend time hanging around the barn. Catherine wondered just what else might be on the menu this morning. Damn the man, he sent one of his minions to argue his case. The thought stiffened her spine.

Molly followed Catherine into the barn. "Do you mind if I watch?" she asked.

Catherine shrugged. "Suit yourself."

Molly could argue from sunrise to sunset, nothing she could say about Billy would change a single thing that had happened. The past was over and done, there was no going back. Catherine's mind was made up where Billy was concerned. If she could retrace her steps magically through time, after meeting the real Billy Raven, all she would change was the depth of her love for him. She would change it to a passing fancy, a momentary infatuation easily forgotten, so their final separation wouldn't have hurt in the least. She would not change their separation. There was nothing for her in Billy Raven's world. His world was the same world she had tolerated for far too long, and then run from.

"I hope the boys and I haven't put you behind schedule," Molly said. "Billy told us how much work you do each day."

"It's okay," Catherine replied, and waited for the other woman to get to the point of her visit. When Molly didn't say anything more, Catherine led the mare down the corridor.

Molly tagged along as Catherine brushed the mare, put her in her stall, and then fed all the other horses. As they moved about the barn, Molly's silence became more and more disconcerting. Finally, Catherine found herself asking, "What do you want, Molly?"

"Just to talk," a slight smile lifted the corners of her mouth, "just to say that Billy is devastated by what happened. In case you can't tell that for yourself."

"I'll have to take your word for it."

Molly gazed at her for a moment. "I really hope you will. I've never seen him as upset as he was after he left here."

"Too bad." Catherine picked up a rope, preparing to lead the stallion out of his stall.

"That's not very charitable of you," Molly said.

Catherine turned on Molly. "You expect me to forgive him, after what he put me through? He made me a laughingstock." Catherine unlatched the stall door and swung it open.

"Nobody is laughing," Molly said.

"Nobody is crying either," Catherine declared over her shoulder.

"I heard you did."

"My brother has a big mouth." Catherine turned toward Molly. "What does Billy want from me this time? Blood?"

"I probably shouldn't tell you this," Molly ran a hand through her untidy hair, "but I think you have the right to know. Billy spent a couple of weeks with us, very upset the whole time. He didn't sleep much."

It seemed that Molly wasn't going to quit, not until she got whatever she was after. If that meant letting Billy off the hook for his lies, Molly was in for a very long day. Catherine had no intention to ignore his behavior. She sighed and put the stallion back in his stall. "No doubt Mr. Raven was suffering from a guilty conscience."

"You can think that, if you like." Molly paused. "Look, can we sit down somewhere?"

Catherine led the way along the corridor and pointed to a stack of hay bales stair-stepping toward the rafters. "Take a seat."

"Thanks." Molly flopped down on one of the bales and leaned back against another one piled behind it. A cloud of dust erupted, swirling through the still air, then drifting slowly away.

Catherine joined her on the makeshift sofa. "Billy is too sure of himself. I can't imagine he would let anything bother him for very long."

"Can't you?" Molly said. "Perhaps you don't know him as well as you think you do."

"I don't know him at all. It was William Caldwell, the handyman, that I thought I knew, and he was just some invention of Billy's imagination."

"No, that's wrong. They are one and the same. William is Billy without the fame."

"You can't separate the two. Not without lying your head off."

"So, the problem between you and Billy comes down to his having lied to you?"

"Of course." Catherine's eyes followed the drifting dust particles as they moved through a shaft of light falling from the window across the corridor.

"Billy told us that he deceived you, but not that he lied to you."

Catherine shook her head. "What else could you call letting me think he needed a job and had no place to live?"

"I might call it the misguided actions of a desperate man."

Catherine turned to stare at Molly. "Sending you here to make excuses for him is another mistake."

Molly shook her head. "It was my idea, not his."

"Do you always butt into other people's lives?" Catherine demanded.

Molly put a gentle hand on Catherine's arm. "Only when I see two people in such obvious pain," she said. "When I love one like a brother and the other seems so hurt it makes me want to throw my arms around her and just hold on."

Catherine pulled away from Molly's touch. "I can take care of myself."

"Everyone can use a friend from time to time."

"You're his friend, not mine."

"I'd like to be yours, too."

With no ready answer, Catherine sat, head bowed, silent and withdrawn. She gazed at her own hands lying slack on her lap. She could feel Molly watching her.

Finally, Molly asked, "Do you know why Billy was driving along that mountain road?"

Without looking up, Catherine shook her head. "Not really. He told me there had been a disagreement over his job, and he confessed that he took the Porsche without asking."

"Disagreement hardly covers it. He thought Cherokee was on the verge of breaking up. Years of hard work threatened to slip out of his grasp."

Catherine turned to look wide-eyed at Molly. "I didn't know."

"Rick told me that Billy and John got into a furious argument. John threw a punch at him, so Billy left the house before tempers got out of hand. And before something was said that couldn't be taken back."

"That's really what happened?" Catherine realized that Billy had told her a simplified version of the truth.

"Yes. So maybe you can understand why Billy is so insistent that you steer clear of John and that you let the rest of us handle his need to stir up trouble. We've all had plenty of practice."

"John isn't a threat to me," Catherine assured her. "In my own way, I've had more practice handling difficult people than any of you have. You should meet my mother, if you doubt me."

Molly gave her a searching look. After a moment she said, "Okay, I believe you."

"Maybe we can be friends, after all." Catherine's ironic tone masked the real emotion behind her remark.

If her relationship with Billy had turned out differently, Molly might have become a good friend. Apart from Maude, who treated her like a granddaughter, Catherine had no close female companions. She had no best friend to share her hopes and fears, no best friend to share her frustrations, either. Suddenly, Catherine's secure world seemed empty and lonely.

Molly fell silent. They sat side-by-side in a golden haze of floating dust and let the peace within the aged barn settle over them. Birdsong drifted in the open door from the trees at the far end of the meadow. The muffled sounds of hooves moving through straw told Catherine that one of her horses had turned in its stall. A stray cat, the color of marmalade, slid from behind the hay bales where they sat and darted down the corridor toward the sunlit stable yard.

Catherine looked down at her hands, and said, "Why didn't he just tell me who he was?"

"What would you have done, if he had?"

Catherine thought about that night, about the near accident and about the storm, and she remembered how drawn to Billy she had been from the first. She weighed other thoughts along with those and answered truthfully. "I would have dropped him off at the first open gas station, or fast food place."

"He told me he fell for you while you were shining a flashlight in his face and threatening to murder him."

Startled, Catherine laughed. "I was worried about the horse trapped in my trailer. I was thinking about broken legs and having to put the horse down. Love was the absolute last thing on my mind."

"Love was the reason Billy became William, the penniless carpenter."

"That's crazy."

"Not so crazy, if the woman you've fallen for hates everything about the kind of life you lead."

Catherine stared at the straw-littered floor and thought about the three days she spent with Billy. She remembered feeling pain and anger and betrayal. She remembered having her heart torn to pieces. She remembered just as clearly the shared moments of tenderness and easy laughter. Could she trust that love had motivated Billy's lies?

Catherine told Molly, "I need to think about this."

Ten

At noon, Catherine walked over to the catering truck. The tables beneath the gaily stripped awning were crowded. The clatter of knives and forks on china mingled with the sound of many conversations. Billy and John sat together, their heads bent over papers spread across the white tablecloth. John pointed to something written on one of the pages and Billy nodded in agreement. Caught up in their discussion, neither man noticed her standing nearby. At another table, Rick inclined his head toward her in greeting and said, "Want some lunch?"

"No, thanks."

At the sound of her voice, John and Billy looked up. John smiled. Billy sat without moving, his face unreadable. Catherine thought it was probably the face he turned toward people who dared to defy him. There was nothing solid in his look, no anger, no hostility of any kind. Just blank nothing. And nothing to fight against. He looked unreachable.

Catherine refused to be put off. She returned John's smile. To Billy, she said, "Can we talk?"

"Why? So you can throw good advice back into my face?" His voice was as unemotional as his expression.

He turned to John. "I think this is a good suggestion. Will you explain it to the director?"

"Sure." John rose from his seat, then winked at her. "See you later, my love."

Catherine shook her head in mock exasperation and grinned at him. "Incorrigible."

"Always." He strode off toward a far table where the director sat surrounded by crew members.

Billy frowned after John. "It's a good thing I love the guy."

"It's a good thing he loves you," she replied. "In some ways you are a lot alike."

Billy looked up at her in surprise. "Not a chance."

Catherine said, "I won't argue with you about it, now. I want to talk about us."

Billy shoved his chair back and stood. "Okay. But not here."

Catherine nodded. "Let's walk out to the meadow."

He collected a handful of sliced carrots from the vegetable tray in the center of the table and handed them to her. "For your four-legged friends."

He dug into a bowl brimming with fresh fruit and grabbed three apples. He stuffed two of them into the pockets of the zippered sweatshirt he wore. He bit into the third apple. "I'm missing lunch."

She pointed to his bulging pockets. "If you're planning to feed those apples to my horses, first you have to cut them into pieces."

He took a knife from the table. "All set. Let's go."

They strolled out of sight of the others and crossed into the meadow. Catherine paused to secure the gate. The heavy chain rattled as she looped it over the gatepost. At the sound, the red mare trotted toward them from the direction of the lake. Catherine laughed. "Here comes Bugs Bunny," she said. "I swear that horse can smell a carrot six miles away."

Catherine set out through the high grass to meet the horse halfway. Billy followed more slowly, enjoying the cool breeze from the lake that ruffled the grass and turned it into a moving green carpet woven through with red clover humming with bees. Beneath the sheltering pines, the grazing horses lifted their heads to watch the mare's meeting with Catherine. Greedy to get at the carrots, the mare first nuzzled Catherine's outstretched hand, then head-bumped her in the chest, knocking her off balance. Billy caught Catherine's arm to steady her.

"Whoa, Bugs." Catherine laughed and shoved the mare's head away. "There's plenty." With the mare trotting at her side, Catherine and Billy strolled together toward the rest of the horses. "Here," Catherine said, sharing the carrots with Billy. Immediately, the mare swung her head in his direction. He pushed the mare's nose away from his fingers, then fed her a piece of carrot.

The two stood in the shade of the pines and handed out the treats to the horses in as fair a way as possible, with the red mare constantly butting in between the others.

Billy sliced one of the apples and fed a piece to Lucky. "I see you still have this guy. Has he gotten any better at jumping?"

"He flies over the jumps like a pigheaded Pegasus. He's still stubborn half the time."

"And that's why you like him," Billy observed. "You like the challenge."

"Maybe so."

Catherine took a piece of apple and held it out to Admiral. The stallion swept the apple off the palm of her hand with the merest brush of his lips. Catherine ran an admiring hand down his silky black neck. He snorted and backed up, suddenly less friendly. Then he moved away and stood in the dense shadows, gazing into the distance, his ears twitching.

Once the horses had finish the carrots and apples, Billy and Catherine sat side-by-side beneath one of the pines. The tree's trunk felt rough against her back, the thick pine straw made a cool cushion beneath her hips. Both the red mare and Lucky lingered nearby, no doubt hoping for more treats. The breeze from the lake brought with it the scent of sun-warmed water plants and the mossy shore. Finches darted among the pine branches, piping small musical notes. "I've been thinking," Catherine began.

"Me, too." Billy took her hand.

"What about?" She turned her head to gaze at him, tempted by his closeness to lay her cheek against his shoulder.

"Stupid mistakes." He shook his head. "Lots of stupid mistakes."

"Yours, or mine?" she asked.

"There are plenty to go around, starting with your brother."

"Oh, yes." She rolled her eyes. "Sin, the puppet master. Sometimes I think he's too much like my mother, when it comes to manipulating people, I mean. Just different motives. He convinces himself that he is helping when he meddles."

"When I found out that you hadn't agreed to lease the farmhouse to us, I was tempted to knock him flat."

"Too bad you didn't," she said. "I've never been more furious with anyone."

"Not true," he said. "You were even angrier with me. I deserved it."

Catherine nodded. "Both of you deserved it, the way you two managed your little conspiracy."

"As I said, we were stupid…and thoughtless."

"Sin was the worst. It doesn't take a mind reader to figure out what he was thinking. Keep Catherine in the dark. Can't wait to see what happens next."

"I flew from Austin to San Francisco just to give him a piece of my mind."

"Really?" Sin hadn't told her that piece of information. "I had no idea."

"After I frightened ten years off his life, I ordered him to keep quiet and let me handle my own affairs. I phoned you several times after that, left half a dozen messages, but you didn't return my calls."

"I was in no mood to talk to you. Now, I see it

would have saved me a lot of anxiety."

"Barging in and invading your privacy was the last thing I wanted to do."

"So why did you?"

"I felt so hopeful when Sin offered us the use of the farm, I thought only about getting back together with you. Not how out of character it would have been for you to agree to his plan."

"Sin can be very persuasive, when he wants to be."

"So can I." Billy's voice was filled with menace.

Catherine turned to look at him. "You didn't hurt him, did you?"

"Hell, no. Just let him think I might. I told him, if he ever fooled with me again, I'd mess up his pretty face." Billy grinned. "You said yourself, I'm a fairly good actor."

"Poor Sin," she said, not sounding sympathetic at all.

Billy laughed. "He'll think twice before he meddles with us again."

"Is there an us?" she asked.

"You know there is." Billy wrapped his arm around her shoulders and pulled her close. "Want me to prove it?"

"I think, yes," she said.

His lips touched her temple, grazed her cheek, and settled over hers. His mouth hovered lazy as a bee in the meadow, sipping, tasting, settling for a long drink. She wrapped her arms around his neck. Oh, yes, she thought, there is definitely something between us.

She kissed him, her kisses wild and free and passionate. She slid her hands inside his open sweatshirt and felt his skin heat beneath her stroking fingers. A low rumble of pleasure rose from his throat. He pulled her across his lap and savaged her mouth.

Minutes later, she pleaded, "Wait, wait, I have to catch my breath."

He smiled down at her. The light in his eyes caught at her heart. "Lady, you take my breath away, too."

She pulled his head down for another kiss, but this time he kept it light. "I thought you wanted to talk," he teased.

She sighed and sat up. "Yes, I think we should."

"Okay. What do you want to talk about?"

"Us. I think we need to talk about what happened between the two of us. I mean, before other people began to interfere."

He snuggled her back into the crook of his arm and ran his fingers through her hair, brushing it off of her face. "I agree. There's still a lot to talk about, even without mentioning Carl and your brother."

"I feel like my life has been flipped upside down, then spun like a top. All because of you."

"My entire existence, my career, and everything that goes with it, has been twisted up like a pretzel, ever since I met you," he said. "I guess we surprised each other."

"That's just it," she said. "Neither one of us has led a normal life since that night on the mountain."

He nodded, thoughtful. "What are you getting at?"

"I think I haven't been quite myself since that first moment. I know that you haven't."

"You mean the Billy-or-William thing, I suppose." He searched her face. "Molly mentioned what you said this morning, about knowing the handyman, but not knowing me."

"It's true. I look at you and see William Caldwell, the unemployed carpenter. I keep expecting you to repair something."

He laughed.

"This is serious," she said.

"Well, that was kind of funny. Sorry."

Catherine waited a moment, then began again. "I trusted William. I thought about my habits and beliefs because of him. Then I found out he didn't exist. I keep asking myself, 'Did I change my whole way of thinking to suit a fantasy?' Does that make any sense at all?"

Billy smoothed a hand over her cheek in a quick caress. "You changed your life months before you met William."

She fell silent, thinking it over. He snuggled her close for a while. When he felt her quiver with checked laughter, he held her away at arm's length and asked, "Now, what's so funny?"

"You're talking about William as if he were someone else. It sounds weird."

"It feels weird. Maybe you should start calling me William," he suggested. "My mother does."

Catherine smiled and shook her head. "I'm not

falling into that trap. She gets exclusive use of her special name for you."

"When she gets mad, she still calls me William Raven Caldwell, as if she plans to send me to my room for a time out."

"Oh, scary!" Catherine giggled.

"Want to trade mothers?" he asked.

"Don't tempt me," she blurted. "Oops, not very loyal, I guess."

"If you ever need a mother, you may borrow mine."

Catherine peered at him. His offer sounded just the slightest bit like a proposal of marriage. Too soon, too soon, a little voice warned from the corner of her mind. She asked, "Are you kidding?"

"No. Come to Austin for a visit. You should meet her."

"I'd love to." Catherine felt relieved that he offered an invitation rather than an engagement ring. "It might clear the cobwebs out of my head. Hearing your mother call you William, I mean."

He tugged at a curl that had drifted across her forehead. "I am he, he is me, and the two of us can't be parted. We like each other too much."

"You're an idiot."

He grinned at her. "Who's the idiot, William, or Billy? I don't know which of us is supposed to be insulted."

She shook her head. "I have no idea. To me, you are two separate people. I guess I have to figure out if I like both of you."

"That's going to be easy to do." He picked up her hand, turned it, and placed a kiss in her palm. His gesture, made familiar by her handyman, warmed her. But she already knew how she felt about William. Her feelings for Billy Raven were the problem.

She turned to face him. "It doesn't feel easy to me. I have no idea how to join your two personalities together to make one man."

"First you kiss William. Then you kiss Billy. And you keep doing that until you can't tell them apart. Of course, I will be in charge of the number of kisses needed for you to come to that conclusion."

Catherine rolled her eyes. "Right now both of you are equally outrageous."

"Apparently, Billy and William have that in common." He smirked at her and she changed the subject.

"Molly said you fell in love with me while I was yelling at you."

"That's what I told her."

"How could that be true? You knew nothing about me at all."

"Love at first sight." He shifted her again to rest on his lap. He sniffed her neck, then placed a tiny kiss there. "You smell good to me."

"I smell like sweaty horses and sun screen most of the time. Listen, I'm not sure I believe in love at first sight. How do you know if what you feel is love, or just hormones?"

"Love, or lust?" His mouth lingered above hers. His warm breath fanned her lips, as he whispered, "Wait and see if it lasts."

Billy kissed her and they feasted like beggars invited to a banquet. They ran their mouths and hands over soft curves and hard muscles, and tugged at unyielding clothes. They tangled their fingers in each other's hair and lay panting side-by-side on a bed of dry pine straw. Billy groaned, "You're killing me."

Catherine turned her head, opened one eye, and gazed at his agonized expression. "Me, too."

Billy said, "We are not going to make love, not until I'm sure we both know what we're doing. But it's getting damn difficult to stop." He levered himself into a sitting position. "I'm full of stickers," he complained, shaking the tail of his sweatshirt. "Now I know why they call them pine needles."

He rose to his feet and extended a hand to her. When she grabbed hold, he hauled her upright and pulled her into an embrace. Catherine wrapped her arms around Billy's waist and strung kisses along his jaw.

"Cut that out," he ordered. "You're going to wreck my self-control."

"That could be interesting," she teased.

"Another time, another place." He freed himself from her grasp and stepped back.

The mare trotted toward them, followed by Lucky. The two horses descended upon Billy, nudging him, investigating his pockets, inhaling the scent of sliced apples clinging to his clothes.

Billy turned toward Catherine, his eyes dancing with laughter.

In the deep shade beneath the trees, the rapid flash of a camera was joined by a man's voice shouting, "Who's the woman, Billy?"

Terrified, the mare bolted for the safety of the meadow. Lucky reared and struck out with his front hooves. One lashing hoof hit the side of Billy's head. Catherine screamed as she watched him fall. His crumpled body seemed to hit the ground in slow motion. He made no sound. Frozen in horror, she screamed again and again, high pitched and hysterical, as the camera wielding intruder danced around Billy's motionless body, snapping picture after picture.

Angry shouts erupted from across the meadow. A crowd of people, John and Carl, and most of the movie crew, vaulted over the gate. The photographer took one look at the mob racing toward him and scrambled away into the underbrush.

John dropped to his knees beside Billy. "Somebody call an ambulance!" he shouted.

"Doing it now," one of the crew yelled, a cell phone to his ear.

Catherine sat wedged between John and Carl in the backseat of a film company car as it sped behind the ambulance. A second car carried Rick, Molly and the twins. Hidden Lake Farm had been left in the possession of the film crew. Catherine wondered briefly what they would do about feeding the horses. Ask her brother, she supposed. She really didn't care.

As the cars raced toward the nearest trauma center at Stanford University Hospital, John and Carl sat in grim silence, offering no words of reassurance. Catherine felt icy cold. Her hands trembled. With her eyes wide open and focused on the rear door of the ambulance speeding ahead of them, all she saw was Billy sprawled in the dirt with blood spilling from his head. The continuous wail of the ambulance's siren had taken the place of her screams.

Two campus police vehicles met them at the entrance to the university. Heads turned as the entourage raced with sirens shrieking through the busy streets leading to the hospital.

The ambulance peeled off and aimed for the emergency department entrance. The two cars carrying the members of Cherokee squealed to a stop in the hospital parking lot. A small group of students and hospital visitors gathered on the sidewalk in front of the main entrance to the building. When one of the students recognized the occupants of the cars, a shout went up, and the little crowd surged toward the band. Campus police moved quickly to head off the onlookers.

John tucked Catherine under his arm and followed Carl and the others through the hospital's front doors, then on to the emergency department. A nurse directed them to an empty office, saying they could wait there without being disturbed by curiosity seekers. The moment the door closed, leaving them alone, Catherine's legs seemed to fail her and she collapsed onto a hard plastic chair. John crouched before her and took her hand. "You look like you're about to faint. Try to breathe slowly. I'll be right back."

He returned with a glass of water and handed it to Catherine. "Here, sip this. If you feel dizzy, put your head down on your knees." He began to pace the room.

An hour passed without interruption by fans, without the return of the helpful nurse, and without any sort of information about Billy. The twins, at first frightened and tearful and clinging to their mother, had become restless. Rick suggested to Molly, "Look, why don't we take the boys for a walk? Find the cafeteria and buy them something to eat. John can call us the minute he hears anything."

After the children had been ushered out of the room, John said, "I don't like this. They should know something by now. We've waited long enough. I'm going to grab hold of a doctor and get a report on Billy's condition."

Carl moved to sit next to Catherine. He draped a huge arm around her shoulders. "I'm staying right here with you," he said.

Catherine nodded and took hold of his hand.

Four hours later, Catherine pushed open the door to Billy's private room. Her heart nearly stopped at the sight of him lying swathed in bandages, in the clutches of a buzzing heart monitor. He hadn't moved or spoken since the accident. The neurosurgeon said he was in a coma and was likely to stay that way until the swelling in his brain began to subside. To her untrained eyes he seemed very deeply asleep.

Even so, she wondered if he might be annoyed by the noisy monitor and couldn't wake himself enough to complain. She'd give anything to hear him bitch about the racket. Then she decided that Billy would be more likely to make some absurd joke about the whole experience.

Tears filled her eyes. Billy's condition was uncertain and nothing to joke about. The doctors had said they couldn't predict when he would wake, or if he would wake at all. They said they preferred not to guess whether he might have brain damage, even if he did regain consciousness. They said all anyone could do was wait and see. They said the next step was up to Billy. They advised her to talk to him, to believe that he could hear her, to believe that somewhere inside his battered body he was simply resting while he healed.

Catherine pulled a tissue from the box on the bedside table and scrubbed at her tears. If Billy's job was to rest and get well, then her job was to talk to him while he did. She drew a chair up close to the bed and ran her fingers over Billy's limp hand. He did not stir. She began telling him about visiting art galleries in Europe, and about meeting an Italian count who thought a wealthy twelve year old American girl would make a suitable wife. That story brought a smile to Catherine's face, a slight smile that soon melted away.

Hours later, Catherine woke. A woman she did not know was crouched beside her chair, watching her as she came awake. Catherine realized that the stranger had said something to her in a quiet voice that had awakened her. She looked at the woman and recognized her face. She wore Billy's chiseled features, softened by femininity and matured by years, and quite lovely. She had Billy's dark hair, or he had hers. Catherine said, "Mrs. Caldwell."

"Please, call me Rebecca." She stood. "And you're Catherine. And my son is very lucky." Catherine jumped to her feet. "No, he's not. If he had never met me, he wouldn't be in this hospital. He wouldn't be hurt. He wouldn't be lying here like this." Tears began to leak from her eyes. "I hate this!"

Rebecca turned to a man standing with his back to the room's closed door. Billy's father said, "You have no reason to blame yourself. But it seems that everyone else is doing the same thing."

Rebecca said, "John thinks it's his fault for not putting guards on the front gate. And Carl thinks it's his fault for barging in on you and Billy without thinking that he might be followed."

Catherine shook her head. "That's nonsense."

"Yes, it is. Still, some of the crew think it's their fault for telling their girlfriends what they would be doing in Northern California, and who they would be doing it for."

Billy's father added, "The only person at fault was the trespasser, who did not come through the front gate, and who probably followed the caterers all the way from Los Angeles."

Catherine said, "I know you're right, Mr. Caldwell. But I can't seem to convince myself that what you say is true."

Rebecca said, "My husband has always been very level headed. You can trust his judgment."

Billy's father planted a kiss on his wife's hand. "Thank you, dearest."

"You're welcome, Matthew."

A multitude of faces were raised toward Billy's hospital window. Every night, night after night, Billy's fans had held candlelight vigils in the parking lot. The campus police, unable to stop them, made a space for the well-wishers in front of the building. The press was relegated to a more distant location, where their trucks, topped by satellite dishes, gave no sign of leaving.

Television reporters, whose faces were familiar to national audiences, camped under plastic canopies strung between their trucks. Catherine watched them as they sat in folding chairs, drinking coffee and eating take-out pizza, and joking among themselves while they waited for news of Billy's death. Nothing less would have kept them near the hospital so long.

John had ordered private security to supplement the campus police and the hospital's own security personnel. His efforts to provide privacy were too late to stop the tabloids. The photos of Billy crumpled on the ground with Catherine standing over him screaming in horror had been splashed throughout the media. Her anguish was emblazoned in magazines, newspapers, and on television gossip shows. She no longer possessed any privacy to protect. Somewhere, in some sunny spot, Catherine imagined, an unscrupulous and newly wealthy photographer had retired to a charming, vine-covered villa, where he reveled in the fruits of his disgusting labors.

As she stared at the crowd below Billy's window, she wondered how any human being could have been so driven by greed that he could profit from the misery of others. Especially if he was the cause of that misery. Catherine shook her head. She would never understand that sort of cowardly evil.

"Come away from that window, Catherine," her mother said. "You're making a spectacle of yourself."

No amount of security, private or otherwise, had managed to keep her mother and father out of Billy's hospital room. Once the news of Catherine's involvement with the rock star became public knowledge, it was inevitable that her parents would have something to say to her about her choice of

236

companions. Within minutes of her parents' arrival, her mother made her disapproval very clear. Her father's thoughts were equally clear. His coldly dismissive glance took in the whole room and everyone in it. He didn't need to say a word to transmit his feelings to Catherine and her friends.

Catherine was grateful to Billy's parents, who, after the briefest of introductions to her mother and father, excused themselves on the pretext of wanting to go to the cafeteria for something to eat. Catherine couldn't help but compare her parents to Billy's, who had spent nearly as much time at his bedside as she had. They lavished her with loving support and never questioned her relationship with their son. Billy's mother had been particularly kind, making sure Catherine rested and kept her spirits up.

Catherine felt deeply ashamed of her own parents as she turned to face them. Her temper was seething, but her expression was bland. She kept her voice low and under control as she asked, "Is that all you have to say, Mother? Does your only concern stem from how I might appear to a bunch of media hacks? Look around. There's an injured man in that bed."

"I think we have all been subjected to quite enough humiliation, because of your affair with this..." Her mother swept an arm in Billy's direction, a disgusted expression twisting her mouth. "...this person. I didn't like his looks from the moment I set eyes on him."

Catherine bit back her first response. Instead, she said, "As I recall, you said you were glad that I had finally taken your advice and hired someone to help me."

Her mother's face grew red. "You deceived me into thinking that he was just some stable boy. A nobody. The two of you must have had a wonderful time laughing behind my back."

"At the time, I didn't know who he was, either," Catherine said.

"Then he made fools of us both. And now, he's dragging our family down to the gutter." Catherine couldn't contain her anger any longer. "Yes, Mother. Like you, I hold this whole disagreeable episode against Billy. After all, he meant all along to be kicked in the head by a panic-stricken horse. And, of course, he must have paid the photographer to snap pictures of him lying on the ground bleeding."

"Be civil," her father said.

"Civil? Why? Have either of you ever shown me the least bit of civility, or sensitivity? When have you cared how I felt about anything?"

"Catherine," her mother glared at her through narrowed eyes, "you are obviously overwrought and don't know what you are saying. I'd advise you to say nothing at all, until you can control yourself."

Catherine stepped toward her mother. "You walk in here uninvited, you have the nerve to criticize and order me around, then expect me to be polite. You are so out of touch with reality, I almost feel sorry for you."

"You will not speak that way to me, ever!" Her mother's voice seemed particularly shrill. Catherine had defied her mother's orders in the past and had been dismissed as an ungrateful, disobedient child. That would not be the outcome today. Catherine smiled.

"I see nothing to smile about, young lady." Her mother began to pace the room. Her high heels striking the floor added a pounding beat to the electronic hum of the bedside monitor. "What did I ever do to deserve such disrespect from my own daughter?"

Catherine laughed out loud. "Oh, don't ask, Mother, don't ask. I can guarantee that you won't like the answer."

Her mother glared at her, then marched to the open door and stood staring down the hall at the bustling nurses' station. Catherine had always known that her mother felt no real fondness for her. What little affection her mother could muster was bestowed on her husband and on his skill as a great artist. The startling thing about her mother's behavior was that her father had done nothing to stop his wife's criticism. Catherine realized that she hadn't seen her parents together that often, not even when she was a child. They were both busy with their careers. Now, she wondered what they were like as a couple. She had trouble imagining either of them anywhere but in a business setting. She couldn't guess what her parents felt for each other. After today, she had no idea if her relationship with them could ever be repaired.

Catherine walked to Billy's bed and touched his hand. Nothing her parents could say compared to the strength of her love for him. She caressed his cheek with her fingertips and smoothed his dark brows. His beautiful long hair was gone now, replaced by stark white bandages. His face was pale, almost the same shade of white as the pillow under his head and the sheet pulled up to his chin. She bent and kissed his lips, then turned toward her parents and said, "I think you had better leave."

Without further argument, her father took her mother by the elbow and steered her from the room. Breathing a sigh of relief, Catherine returned to stare out of the window. The crowd had grown in the gathering dusk. A sliver of moon hung low in the sky. Stars must be there, too, she thought, but the city lights washed out their distant shining. The night sky looked far brighter above the farm. She wished she could show the stars to Billy. She hoped she would get that chance before too long. She loved him so much, maybe her love would reach him and wake him from his sleep.

She pressed her forehead against the cool window glass. The constant presence of fans in front of the hospital, standing watch near Billy's room, was a sign of their love and loyalty. A country music fan all her life, a taste acquired from fellow horse trainers, Carl was the one who introduced her to Cherokee's music.

The morning after Billy's accident, Carl arrived at the hospital carrying a complicated piece of electronics, the kind you can't buy off the shelf at a big box store. The thing could play any of Cherokees's songs in any order, and could be adjusted in a dozen different ways to modify the music to fit the whim of the one listening. Carl insisted that Billy would awaken from his coma sooner, if he heard familiar music playing. Catherine took one look at the electronic marvel and asked which of the many controls was the on/off button. Carl set the playlist in chronological order and let the music softly fill the room. Since then, Catherine and Carl had become close friends, spending many worrisome hours together at Billy's bedside, playing the songs over and over again, while Billy slept on and on.

Now, with Cherokee's music playing in the background, she moved to stand by his bedside and looked down at him. How relaxed he seemed. How peaceful. Perhaps he dreamed. She couldn't tell by looking at him. From time to time during the past week, he had moved in his sleep. Each time he did, Catherine hoped he would wake and smile up at her. The doctors had explained that these movements were normal, and not a sign that Billy was coming out of his coma. They weren't a sign of anything in particular, so she shouldn't get her hopes up. Still, she stood over him, wishing that he would move again, willing him to wake up.

After watching him sleep for a while, Catherine pulled the hospital armchair close to the bed and sat down. She shut her eyes, trying to calm her restless thoughts, and listened to Billy's voice drifting from the electronic marvel. Billy had written the lyrics and had composed most of the music. She had listened to the songs so many times, day after day, she knew all of the words by heart. She began to sing along.

"Off key," a whispery voice said.

"Oh, my God!" Catherine leaped out of the chair. "You're awake, you're awake. Oh, thank God!"

Eleven

AFTERWORD

Sin came to sit beside Catherine on the porch of the newly renovated house. The wicker chair creaked as he leaned back and settled his bare feet on the carved wooden railing that had been lovingly restored to its original condition and painted forest green. Catherine followed his example and propped her bare feet beside his. She wiggled her toes to admire the whimsy her brother had created. Instead of her usual pale pink polish, her toenails glowed with tiny pictures of rainforest frogs. The project had been her brother's way of helping her pass the time. This particular afternoon, she was as restless as Sin was calm and relaxed.

She looked across at the barn. Sin's artistic skills had been at work there, as well. The building oozed Elizabethan charm. Her brother's infallible eye combined function with historical authenticity and romance. Cream colored stucco covered the old wooden walls and filled the spaces between heavy, crossed timbers stained a rich chocolate brown. Composed as carefully as one of their father's masterpieces, the refurbished barn was topped by a genuine thatched roof. Her brother's love of all things Irish included the scarlet climbing roses that flanked the barn's roughhewn double doors. The long, curved driveway had been paved with cobblestones. In the past year, Sin and his team of artisans and construction workers had performed miracles.

The abandoned house had become a gracious home under his hands. Color brought cheer to the rooms. The new kitchen, a marvel of technology, challenged Catherine to prepare meals worthy of the professional appliances. She longed for the skill to do it, but had to settle for an occasional mac and cheese casserole. Sin's studio had been expanded into a generous, sun-filled loft. The remaining space upstairs contained two master bedroom suites, each with its own spa-like bathroom, Sin's in teal and white tile, with black trim, and Catherine's in sea green tile, with touches of gold.

The living room no longer held lingering ghosts. Filled with antiques and contemporary pieces, the room welcomed visitors with warmth, and offered comfort along with serenity. Two of their father's landscapes faced each other from opposite walls. A portrait of Sin and herself as children, holding calico kittens in their hands, hung over the fireplace. It no longer mattered to Catherine that the kittens had been borrowed for the occasion. One thing remained unchanged. She turned her head and gazed at the massive front door that William, the unemployed carpenter, had repaired to earn his keep. The redwood glowed under a protective coat of fresh varnish. Wind and rain could not harm it.

Past the door, at the far end of the porch, new hardware replaced the rusted chains of the old swing. Cozy pillows in rainbow hues lined its back. One of the half-tame barn cats slept there in a patch of sunlight, oblivious to the presence of the homeowner and his sister. Catherine let her head fall onto the back of her wicker chair as she, too, closed her eyes. She and Sin had shared the spacious house for several months, after he gave up his penthouse in San Francisco, and lured her out of her tiny apartment in the barn. She smiled, remembering how little enticement it had taken to get her to move, once she saw her new bedroom suite with its luxurious bathroom.

Furnished differently, her old apartment in the barn now served as her office, a necessity due to increased business. Accustomed to the perversity of her fellow human beings, Catherine had managed to remain detached and calm when the notoriety of Billy's accident brought her several offers to train horses. She turned down every one of these offers without comment, just as she had rejected the many invitations to tell her story to the curious audiences of television talk shows. On the other hand, horse owners and trainers she had known most of her life had rallied around her, caring for her horses during the first few hectic days spent at the hospital, when she had been consumed with worry over Billy. Once he was out of danger, she accepted referrals from people she thought of as guardian angels. Her newly renovated stable had filled with horses. So many horses that Catherine found it necessary to hire an assistant.

The girl handled Admiral as if he were a merry-go-round pony. Her high spirits matched the high energy of the stallion, making it a pleasure to watch the two at work in the exercise ring.

Catherine lazed in the sunshine and let her thoughts drift. She refused to dwell on her mother and father, and on her disappointment in them. Someday, perhaps, she would reconcile with them. She felt no pressure to correct the situation any time soon. She had her own life to live, and live in a way that pleased herself. Her self-doubt had disappeared once she admitted that tying herself into knots trying to satisfy others was a poor substitute for behaving like an adult. Her days had become tranquil and satisfying. Her love for Billy had grown. Her future seemed blessed.

She felt the sun on her face and knew contentment.

Sin reached for the pitcher of lemonade on the table between their chairs. Ice cubes rattled from the pitcher into his glass as he poured himself a second helping. Catherine opened her eyes and held out her empty glass. "Me, too, please," she said.

Sin filled her glass and handed it to her. She took a sip. "Thanks."

On the table beside the frosted pitcher, a tall vase held two dozen yellow roses. Catherine touched the softness of one blossom, then plucked the card from their midst. She read the message once more, a slight smile playing at her lips.

"Billy will be here soon," her brother said.

"Yes."

"Are you going to marry him?" Sin stared at her, worry sketching lines between his brows.

She nodded. "If he asks."

"Your life won't be easy," Sin warned.

Catherine had flown to Texas several times during the past year. Each time, staying with Billy and his parents while he recovered from his injuries. "We've gotten to know each other very well," she said. "It will be all right."

"What about the press? And all of Billy's fans? They'll never give you a moment's peace."

"We've talked it over. More than once. It's not as if I don't know what to expect. Our parents weren't exactly anonymous, you know."

"That was them, loving the spotlight. This is you, hating the spotlight. And Billy, who has a lot of reasons to want to avoid calling attention to himself."

"The press got such a black eye from that photographer's disgraceful behavior, most have been very thoughtful ever since. The first time Billy and I went out in public together, a couple of photographers asked us if they each could, please, take just one picture."

She laughed. "The poor things looked as if they were ready to run away, if Billy frowned at them."

Sin just looked at her and didn't join in the laughter. He seemed single-minded in his attempt to challenge Catherine's view of the future. He asked, "What about all those screaming kids?"

"What about them?"

"They're not at all like the people who go to mother's book signings. There's a reason that the word fan is short for fanatic. Without much encouragement, they can turn into a barely controlled mob."

"That mob stood watch with me at the hospital. They love Billy and, for that, I love them. Billy is planning a thank you concert at Stanford in the next month, or so. I'm looking forward to meeting as many of his mob of fans as I can."

Her brother's troubled gaze studied her face. "You're sure?"

She smiled at him. "Positive."

Sin continued to stare at her. Finally, he said, "As long as it's what you want, then it's okay with me."

Catherine read the message written on the florist's card again, then slid the card back among the roses. "It's what I want. Billy is the man I want. He makes me happy. I feel content when we're together."

"Okay." Her brother swung his feet off of the porch rail and stood looking down at her. "I've got to go back to work. Send Billy up to the studio when he gets here."

"Why?" she scoffed. "So he can ask you for my hand in marriage?"

"Not a chance. I quit meddling in your life a year ago."

"Good thing. Somebody might get mad at you, someday." She narrowed her eyes at him and pursed her lips.

He held up his hands palms out. "I have reformed, completely, absolutely."

Smiling, she said, "Time will tell."

He shrugged. "So. Send him up. I want to say hello."

"Wait your turn," she told him.

A half hour later, a shiny black truck swung up the curving, cobblestone-paved drive. The brand new pickup stopped beside the line of dark green shrubs, thick with fragrant white gardenias, that formed a barrier between the front lawn and the driveway. At the sound of the truck's door slamming, Catherine's heart began to pound.

Billy moved up the path toward the porch, his gaze first caressing her face, then holding steady, looking into her eyes. "Hi," he said. Catherine thought his smile held enough light to banish the darkness of the world. He paused at the top of the steps, taking in the barn cat curled in the sunshine in the center of the porch swing, then he came to her and sat on the rail beside her bare feet.

He touched one of the little frogs. "Cute toes." When his hand traveled across her foot and grasped her ankle, she shivered. His fingers stroked upward from her ankle past her knee. His hand wasn't quite steady as it reached the hem of her cutoff denim shorts, before retreating. She smiled up at him.

"You got the flowers," he noted.

"Yesterday."

"One dozen from William the handyman, one dozen from me."

"Thank you, it was a lovely gesture."

Billy surveyed the renovations to Hidden Lake Farm. "Want to show me around?" She rose from the wicker chair. "I'll put on some shoes," she told him, then passed into the house without touching him.

He stood leaning against one of the pillars that supported the porch roof, waiting for her return. Soon the time of waiting would end. During the last long year, all of them had changed. He had. Catherine, too. The members of the band. Even George and Henry. A year older, now, the twins seemed a head taller and even more energetic. He had visited them just last week at Rick and Molly's new place outside of Austin. They had purchased the red mare from Catherine's client, and bought a small ranch with a large barn to stable her in. The boys rode bareback like little Cossacks, and whooped with laughter when asked why they renamed their aristocratic, red Thoroughbred Bugs Bunny.

Billy smiled. With Catherine's expert help, he'd buy another equally patient horse for the twins, to give Bugs a break, so she didn't have to haul around both boys at the same time.

Catherine returned, wearing jeans and boots. Earlier in the year she had cut her hair very short, as a show of solidarity with Billy's hospital-shaved head. She no longer covered her curls with a bandana. During her first trip to Austin to visit Billy, he ran his fingers through her hair, fluffing it every which way, and dubbed her Curly. He delighted in the nickname, and introduced her to friends in an exaggerated drawl that made her think of old-time western movies, and made everyone laugh.

Today, as she reached his side, he tousled her hair and said, "Give me a kiss, Curly." She grinned at him. "I thought you wanted a tour of the farm. You didn't say anything about kissing."

In the same overdone Texas drawl, he said, "Just one little peck for this lonesome cowboy before we stroll through that meadow full of horse poop on our way to the lake."

He pulled her into his arms and claimed her mouth in a stunning act of possession that left her breathless. "Wow," she said, when the porch floor stopped tilting under her feet.

"Plenty more where that one came from," he promised.

"Let's walk, before I embarrass myself on my brother's front porch," she replied.

Billy took her hand and led her down the steps.

She leaned her head against his shoulder as they ambled past the rose-covered barn and far into the meadow. They reached the lakeshore and stood there for a while. The sun rode low in the sky, casting a golden glow onto the lake's surface. The colors of sunset deepened into countless shades of blue as Billy and Catherine followed the trail around the lake toward the grassy hideaway on the opposite shore. Much had happened there with her carefree car thief handyman, and with the renowned rock star holding her hand and walking at her side.

I   n the first weeks after Billy was released from the hospital, they had come many times to the lakeshore to sit and absorb the peace. To heal. The sheltered cove held a thousand memories for Catherine. This evening, she knew that Billy intended to add one very special memory to the others, a memory to cherish in her heart of hearts. She followed him gladly.

They sank to the grass, their backs against the rock that resembled a stone troll. He smiled at her. "How's it been, living with your brother?"

"Surprisingly easy," she said. "And entertaining, watching him try out the role of landscape gardener. He's been filling the flower beds with plants that bloom in intricate patterns of contrasting colors."

Billy laughed. "Sin with a shovel in his hand instead of a paintbrush. That must be something to see."

"Yes, it is." Catherine snuggled closer to Billy's side. "How have you been?"

"Clean bill of health," he smiled.

"I'm thankful for that. You have no idea how awful you looked in the hospital."

He grinned at her. "Not true. Carl took a picture."

"He didn't!"

"Yep. But this one won't appear in any tabloids. He had it framed for me as a souvenir."

"I think I will have a talk with Carl about his sense of humor."

"You can swear at him in French. Maybe you know some naughty words he doesn't."

She chuckled. "Good idea."

Billy brought her hand to his lips and kissed her fingertips one by one.

"I love your gentleness," she told him. "Somehow, even in the midst of all our arguments, I recognized that part of you from the start."

He shook his head. "Except for that one argument about John. I was out of line. And it turned out that you were right about him. He respects you, and would never hurt you."

"You would never hurt me either, no matter how angry you got."

Billy turned her hand over and kissed the palm. "I love you," he said. "So much that I hardly know myself anymore."

"I know you. You are my best friend."

"Could you see yourself marrying your best friend?" He asked the question her heart and soul had waited so patiently to hear.

She framed his face between her hands and placed a tender kiss on his lips. The kiss he gave her in return set her heart afire.

Billy took her hands in his, keeping her from touching him, when all she wanted to do was touch him. "What if reporters leap out of the bushes and snap pictures of you in your underwear?"

She smiled. "I'll buy new underwear. A different color every week. That way, when the pictures show up in the tabloids, we'll know when the photos were taken."

"I'll get copies and hang them on my recording studio walls."

She tipped her head back and gave him a mock frown. "If you do, I'll get Sin to paint you in the nude."

He laughed. "Don't give me ideas. Particularly such a good one."

"I will never, I repeat, never pose naked in front of my brother."

"Damn. You've destroyed just about the best fantasy I've ever had."

She leered at him. "Any other fantasies I ought to know about, before I answer?"

"I have enough money for six lifetimes. Maybe I'm planning to let you work to support me, while I raise our kids." He tweaked her nose between his fingers.

"Really?"

He nodded. "Most of the time," he said.

"I don't believe it."

"Trust me. The band's going to cut back on touring. Rick and Molly are pretty happy about that decision, I can tell you." He ruffled her hair. "This morning I made an offer on sixty acres just beyond the lake. It's a piece of property, I might add, brought to my attention by an overzealous photographer. It's going to be you and me, Curly. And a bunch of kids. And about eight hundred horses, if I know you."

"What if I say no?"

"If you say no, you'll be here training horses, and I'll be next door raising rattlesnakes." She kissed his neck and whispered a single word in his ear.

His arms tightened around her and he carried her with him down to the deep grass.

Much later, they walked back to the house in the moonlight.

The End